BOSSY

LITTLE DIDDUMS

POLICE DOG DEPENDABLE

MUMMY

DADDY

£1.00

The Jolly Dogs

Hundreds of thousands of children everywhere have met the Jolly Dogs already. They first appeared in a splendid series of stories in that popular weekly paper "Once Upon a Time."

The stories were written by Barbara Hayes and the pictures were drawn by W. Francis (Bill) Phillipps. These two very talented people had collaborated some years previously in creating ever-famous Teddy Bear of "Teddy Bear Weekly." Seeking something new Barbara Hayes devised the Jolly Dog Family — Mummy and Daddy, Gay Dog, Bossy, Hero and Little Diddums — and all the other amusing folk of Dogsville, Police Dog Dependable, Husky Dog, Dog Watch, Dog Tired, Sly Dog and several others.

Some of the "Once Upon A Time" stories are re-presented here. There are also new stories especially written for this book.

Children and parents will share the fun of these happy stories. Turn the pages and start laughing — for **"The Jolly Dogs have arrived!"**

Published by Ideabooks, 72 Lower Addiscombe Road Croydon, Surrey, England. Printed by Varnicoat Ltd., Pershore, Worcestershire. © Ideabooks.

ISBN 0 85988 003 6

The Jolly Dogs
OF DOGSVILLE

Stories by
Barbara Hayes

Pictures by
W. Francis Phillipps

IDEABOOKS

Daddy

Gay Dog

Hero

The Jolly Dogs

Little Diddums

Mummy

Bossy

CHAPTER 1

Ha! Ha! Ha!
How everyone was laughing!
It was always like that when Gay Dog was around.

"What does a horse become after it is eight years old?" Gay Dog asked his sister Bossy.

"Oh, I'll never guess!" gasped Bossy.

"*Nine* years old!" laughed Gay Dog.

Then Gay Dog looked at his brother Hero.

"What runs round the house but never moves an inch?" he asked.

Hero shook his head.

"A fence!" chuckled Gay Dog.

Then Gay Dog looked at his smallest brother — Mummy's Little Diddums.

"What is the last thing you take off when you go to bed?" Gay Dog asked Diddums.

Diddums thought and thought.

"Oh, I don't know," he said.

"Your feet off the floor," grinned Gay Dog.

Then Gay Dog told the other dogs in his family about how he had just met a friend of his who had got a new job.

"My friend told me he had ten dogs working under him," said Gay Dog, "so I said, 'Oh I suppose you are the boss then?' 'No,' said my friend, 'I'm working on the roof and the other ten are in the house.'"

"Ha! Ha! Ha!"

Everyone laughed again.

Things were always jolly when Gay Dog was around.

That was how he got his name — because he was such fun.

Anyway, just then Gay Dog had to go to work at the car salesrooms, but before

he left, he said to his family: "I've bought myself something really nice. You look out for me when I come home this evening and you will see what it is."

Of course, all day long the dogs — Mummy and Daddy and Hero, the middle brother, and Bossy, the only girl, and Mummy's Little Diddums, the dog with the sweet nature — were bursting with curiosity to know what Gay Dog had bought.

And then in the evening they found out.

Gay Dog drove home in a beautiful, new, red sports car.

"What do you think of this, then?" beamed Gay Dog proudly, as he pulled up by the front garden gate.

Well, of course, everyone thought the car was lovely.

But then Daddy Dog said:

"Where are you going to keep it, Gay Dog? We have only one garage and my van is in there."

You see, Daddy Dog kept a Dog Biscuit shop and he had to have a van for delivering the biscuits to his customers.

For a moment Gay Dog looked a little worried.

"Well, it's like this, Dad," he said, shifting from one foot to the other and looking down at the ground and up at the sky and anywhere, except straight at his father.

"In a few days — that is — in a week — well, maybe in a couple of weeks — let's call it a month — old Mr. Towser, who lives next door but one, will be able to let me use *his* garage. But until then, I wondered if you would mind if *I* used *our* garage and *your* van stood out in the road . . ."

Gay Dog's voice trailed away, because he knew he was really being rather cheeky.

Then he went on quickly:

"You see, I thought — well, Dad's van is very old and rather scratchy and if it gets a bit wet out in the rain or if anyone scratches it or bangs it — well, it won't matter all that much. But my car is nice and new and it would be a shame if anything happened to it — so I thought good old Dad won't mind if my car goes into the garage for a day or two — that is

for a week — well, maybe a couple of weeks — well, let's call it a month . . ."

All the dog family stood looking at Gay Dog in silence.

Then Bossy, who always believed in saying exactly what she thought, said:

"What you mean is you want your car to go into the garage because it's *yours* and you think a lot of it — and you want *Dad's* van to stand out in the rain, because it's *Dad's* and you don't care what happens to it."

There was another silence while everyone looked at everyone else.

Then good old Dad said:

"Well, I don't mind if my van stands in the road for a night or two — after all it *is* old and it would be a shame if Gay Dog's lovely new sports car was spoilt."

Gay Dog looked relieved.

"You're a real sport, Dad," he said.

"Sport! Huh!" snapped Bossy. "Dad's just being soft with you as usual — he

always is with you boys. Now if it had been my car, it would have been mighty different, I can tell you."

Little Diddums looked at Bossy in surprise.

"But you haven't *got* a car!" he said.

"Oh, shut up!" snapped Bossy, who was rather jealous of Gay Dog's car and felt in a grumpy mood.

Now Bossy was also jealous because she had always wanted to have the garage as a play room, and Daddy wouldn't let her.

"Oh no — *I'm* not good enough to have the garage," she thought to herself, "but Gay Dog and his fancy red car are good enough — oh, dear me, yes."

Bossy watched Daddy take his van out of the garage and park it in the road.

Then she watched Gay Dog put his lovely new red sports car in the garage.

"I'm not going to take this lying down," she thought. "I'm going to make trouble."

CHAPTER 2

Bossy gets difficult

The very first night that Daddy left his van out in the road all night, Bossy got up early and crept over to the window to look out.

"Daddy! Daddy!" shrieked Bossy, rushing and banging on her Daddy's bedroom door. "I thought you left your car parked by the front gate!"

"I did! I did!" gasped poor Daddy waking up from a deep sleep and leaping out of bed in alarm.

Of course, he thought that Bossy was going to say that the car wasn't there any more.

But naughty Bossy, as soon as she saw that she had woken everyone up, grinned slyly to herself and said:

"Well, I thought you would like to know that it is still there."

"Oh, Bossy! You really are the limit!"

groaned Gay Dog stumbling out of his bedroom and dragging on his dressing gown and slippers. "You knew that when we all heard you shouting like that we should think that something was wrong! Fancy waking us up at this time in the morning."

Bossy grinned.

"I said I would cause trouble all the while your car was parked in Daddy's garage, and cause trouble I will," she said to Gay Dog. "Now see if you can make one of your jokes about that!"

My goodness, Bossy was being difficult, wasn't she?

Mummy's Little Diddums, the youngest dog, who had a very sweet nature, said:

"As Bossy is being naughty, I will try to be extra good to make up. I will go and make toast for everybody and bring it up

to them in bed to make up for Bossy's having woken them so early."

"Traitor!" snapped Bossy, giving Diddums a very nasty look as he went past.

But Diddums was so sweet, he didn't bear any grudge against Bossy.

In fact, he brought her up toast in bed as well and even put extra butter and jam on her slice.

"I know you are only being nasty because you are upset and jealous," said Diddums to Bossy, "so I forgive you."

"Oh, shut up!" snapped Bossy.

But she took the toast and ate it.

Anyway, the day went on its usual way, until supper time came round again.

Then as the family sat around eating, with Gay Dog's new red sports car in the garage and Daddy's van standing out in the road, Bossy started again.

"I hear a lot of cars have been stolen lately," she said. But as nobody replied, she went on, "What would happen if someone stole Daddy's van? After all, it would be very easy to steal, standing out in the road like that."

Daddy Dog looked up.

"I say! That is a thought," he said. "If someone stole my van, it would be very difficult for me to carry on with my work at the Dog Biscuit shop. I should have nothing to deliver the biscuits in."

Bossy started to grin.

"Then," she said, "the best thing is for Gay Dog's car to stand in the road and for your van to go back into the garage."

But Daddy wouldn't have that.

"I promised Gay Dog his car could stay in the garage, and stay in the garage it will," he said.

Then he went on: "Anyway, let's stop all this talk of car stealing. We'll all have a good night's sleep and forget about cars."

So they did — and in the morning, there was Daddy's van standing at the curbside safe and sound.

But my goodness what a shouting and a roaring there was when Gay Dog opened the garage door.

"My car! My lovely car!" shrieked Gay Dog.

Bossy pricked up her ears and ran out.

"Don't tell me your car has been stolen from out of the garage," she said, grinning hopefully.

"No it hasn't been stolen," shouted Gay Dog. "But just look at it!"

"It's all muddy!" gasped Hero.

"Oh, Gay Dog, I am so sorry!" said Mummy's Little Diddums, giving Gay Dog's paw a squeeze.

"It looks as if it has been out in the rain!" cried Mummy.

"It looks as if someone has driven it for miles along muddy lanes!" said Daddy.

"But it's been locked in the garage all night," shouted Gay Dog, fairly dancing with fury. "How could it have got into this dreadful state?"

Then he turned and glowered at Bossy.

"*You* have done this, I know you have!" he snorted.

Bossy grinned back.

"No, I didn't do it," she said, "I would have done if I'd thought of it, but I didn't think of it — worse luck!"

Who had been responsible for making Gay Dog's car so dirty? There were to be lots of exciting adventures ahead.

CHAPTER 3

A CASE FOR
Police Dog

She began arguing as to how Gay Dog's car became dirty, until Daddy Dog finally said:

"Well, if the car has been locked in the garage all night, then you must have made it dirty before you put it away last night, Gay Dog. That's all I can say — and now I must get on with my work."

So the arguing stopped, and all the dogs went about their daily business.

During his lunch hour, Gay Dog made sure that he cleaned his car until there wasn't a speck of dirt or mud on it anywhere.

That evening before he locked it away in the garage he made the whole family look at it.

"It is as clean as a new pin, isn't it?" he said, "so if it's dirty in the morning, no one can say that it was dirty when I put it away."

The next morning all the dog family were awake early.

Gay Dog took the key of the garage from under his pillow, where it had been all night, and ran out to the garage.

He unlocked the door and looked in at his car.

"Oh, *no!*" he groaned.

"It's happened again!" chuckled Bossy.

"What a shame!" said dear Little Diddums and he went indoors to tell Mummy Dog to make poor Gay Dog a cup of tea to help him get over the shock.

For there in the garage, was Gay Dog's lovely red sports car with mud splashed over it from end to end — just as if it had been driven for miles over rough, muddy, country lanes.

Gay Dog staggered indoors and couldn't say a word until he had drunk his tea with three extra lumps of sugar in it.

Clatter, clatter, clatter!

The cup and saucer rattled against each other as Gay Dog put them down on the table with a shaking paw.

"I shall have to call the police," he muttered, "there is something very mysterious going on here."

Police Dog Dependable was just having breakfast down at the police station, when the phone rang.

"What's up now?" he said to himself. "When the phone rings as early as this, it means trouble."

Police Dog Dependable picked up the phone, and was pleased when he found that he was talking to Gay Dog.

"I heard a good joke the other day," he said. "I know how you like jokes, Gay Dog, so I was saving it to tell to you. It was about two boys who were late for school. 'Why are you late?' the teacher asked the first boy. 'I dreamed I was going to America,' said the first boy. 'And why are *you* late?' the teacher asked the second boy. 'I dreamed I was seeing him off!' said the second. Ha! Ha! Ha!"

How Police Dog Dependable laughed.

But then he looked more serious as Gay Dog didn't laugh very much and started telling him about his car.

"You want to report trouble with your car, do you?" he asked. "Has it been stolen, then?"

Police Dog Dependable opened his note-book and licked his pencil. He listened to what Gay Dog was telling him over the phone and his eyebrows shot up.

"It hasn't been stolen — and you want to complain because it's *dirty*!"

Then Police Dog Dependable spoke kindly into the telephone.

"Now just listen, Gay Dog. If everyone in this town who had a dirty car, rang me up and complained about it, my phone would never stop ringing. I'm sorry your lovely car has got dirty, but that's life, you know. You'll just have to clean your car like the rest of us do, and make the best of it."

And Police Dog Dependable rang off and got on with eating his breakfast.

Back in the dog family's home Gay Dog put down the receiver of the telephone.

"Well, what did Police Dog say?" asked Mummy Dog.

"He says if my car gets dirty, then I must clean it like everyone else," said Gay Dog.

"But didn't he understand that your car got dirty inside a clean, locked garage?" asked Daddy Dog. "Police Dog is usually a very understandable chap."

"At this hour in the morning *and* before breakfast, I don't think *anyone* would understand that!" said Gay Dog and sat looking gloomily at his empty tea cup.

Then Bossy, who was beginning to feel sorry about all her nasty jealousy about Gay Dog's car, decided to try to do something to help.

"Why don't we ask Watch Dog to help us?" she asked. "He likes sitting up all night watching things. He is a chum of mine and I know he would love to sit up all night watching your car to see how it gets so dirty."

"What a super idea!" said Gay Dog. "Could you fix it for me, Bossy?"

So Bossy did.

And that night, when all the Dog family settled down for the night, Watch Dog sat in the front parlour window watching the doors of the garage.

CHAPTER 4

TICK-TOCK TICK-TOCK TICK-TOCK

Now Watch Dog earned his living by watching things—like holes in the road or valuable jewellery or cars.

But, as well as that, Watch Dog was called Watch Dog because he loved watches and wore lots and lots of them up and down his arms.

Tick—tock! Tick—tock! Tick—tock!

You could always tell when Watch Dog was near by the sound of all his watches ticking.

Well, the dog family—Mummy and Daddy, Gay Dog the grown-up son, Hero, the half-grown-up son, Bossy the little girl, and the baby of the family, Mummy's Little Diddums, who was such a sweet little puppy, all settled down to sleep.

And in the parlour window sat Watch Dog, watching and waiting to see what would happen to the car.

Suddenly Watch Dog heard some stealthy footsteps creeping towards him.

He picked up the big stick he always kept at his side on dark nights.

The footsteps came nearer and nearer, and then, by the light of the moon, Watch Dog saw Bossy push open the door and come into the room.

"Have you seen anything yet?" she hissed.

Watch Dog put down his stick.

"No!" he hissed back.

"With all the tick—tocking of your watches disturbing me, and being all excited, I couldn't sleep," went on Bossy, "so I thought I would come down and help you with your watching."

So for a while Bossy and Watch Dog sat looking out of the parlour window together, watching the locked doors of the garage.

But Bossy seemed a bit restless.

She kept glancing at the covered plate on the table.

"They were super sandwiches Mummy left for you," she said. "I helped her to make them, so I know."

Watch Dog stretched out an arm and glanced at about six watches.

"Oh, yes, it is supper time," he smiled.

"Would you like to share a sandwich with me, Bossy?"

"I was beginning to think you'd never ask," grinned Bossy, reaching out her paw and taking the sandwich that she knew had the thickest slice of ham in it.

But then, suddenly, as the two dogs were happily chomping away, Watch Dog caught his breath and leaned forward.

"There's someone slinking up the road," he said. "I just saw someone dodge from one shadow to another on the opposite pavement."

Bossy peered out of the window.

Sure enough, in a moment, she saw a slim, crouchy figure slip from the shadow of a tree into the shadow of a bush near their own garden.

"I think it's time to creep outside now," said Watch Dog, "so that we can see what is really happening."

They padded softly along the black shadow at the side of the garden fence, until they were standing quite close to the garage—just where they could see, but where they could not be seen.

But, by golly, although they could not be seen, they could certainly be heard.

Tick-tock! Tick-tock! Tick-tock!

In the stillness of the night, every one of Watch Dog's watches sounded as loud as someone hammering nails into a piece of wood!

"We might just as well sit here banging a big drum as sit here with all your watches ticking," grumbled Bossy to Watch Dog. "You should have left them behind in the house, you blockhead!"

Watch Dog was rather annoyed.

"Now look here, don't talk to me like that, Miss Bossy ..." he said. "ULP!"

Two furry figures suddenly jumped out on Watch Dog and grabbed him by the arms.

"Sssssh!" puffed the furry figures. "It's only us!"

Peering through the darkness, Watch Dog saw Hero and Mummy's Little Diddums, Bossy's two brothers.

They each held a pillow and they were holding the pillows over Watch Dog's arms, so that they muffled the sound of the watches ticking.

"We saw you creep out, so we came to join you," they hissed. "Weren't we clever to think of bringing the pillows to keep the watches quiet?"

Then suddenly all four dogs froze.

The same slim figure that Watch Dog had seen before slunk out of the shadows and crept towards the garage doors.

For a moment, the moonlight shone full on his face. ·

Hero caught his breath.

"I know who that is," he gasped. "It's SLY DOG!"

An Exciting Chase

CHAPTER 5

Watch Dog, Bossy, Hero and Little Diddums all stood there silently watching Sly Dog as he fiddled with the lock of the garage door.

Sly Dog wore rather shabby clothes and soft shoes and he had a rather long twitchy nose and all the time he kept glancing to and fro and over his shoulder to see if anyone was watching him.

"So that's Sly Dog, is it?" muttered Watch Dog, "I've often heard about him and the sly way he tries to cheat and trick people."

The dogs went on watching, until they saw Sly Dog click open the lock of the garage, push the doors open and slip inside.

"How clever to be able to open a garage without having a proper key!" said Mummy's Little Diddums, who always tried to see good in everyone.

"Oh shut up!" snapped Bossy, looking down at her baby brother. "Opening somebody else's garage doors is *sneaky*, not *clever*!"

Diddums was hurt at being snapped at.

"Well I'm only Mummy's Little Diddums. How was I supposed to know?" he whimpered.

Just then Watch Dog stepped forward into the moonlight.

"Well, it's time to tackle Sly Dog and ask him what he's doing in your father's garage," he said.

But Bossy grabbed at Watch Dog and held him back.

"No!" she said. "If we catch Sly Dog, he will never tell us the truth. Let us just follow him and see what he does."

"How can we follow him?" said Watch Dog. "If he drives off in Gay Dog's brand new sports car we shall never be able to catch him."

"Oh, for heaven's sake!" gasped Bossy. "We can follow him in Daddy's old van. I just happen to have brought the keys along with me from off Daddy's dressing table."

But Watch Dog wasn't doing anything like that.

"I am a *watch* dog," he said, "not a chase-across-the-countryside-in-someone-else's-car dog. Now, young Diddums, you just cut along back indoors and wake up your Dad and your big brother Gay Dog. Tell them that we've got Sly Dog bottled up in the garage and what do they want done about it?"

And Diddums, who was always a good boy and did as he was told, padded back to the house as fast as he could go.

Bossy was disgusted.

"What a weak kneed lot you are!" she sneered. "Just when there is a chance of some real excitement, you have to run to fetch the grown-ups."

But then suddenly Watch Dog and Hero and Bossy stared in astonishment.

Rolling out of the garage, without making a sound, came Gay Dog's lovely new red sports car.

"However did that happen?" gasped Hero.

Then they saw that on the other side of the car was Sly Dog, heaving hard. He had taken off the brakes and was pushing the car down the slope to get it away from the the house before he started the engine.

That way, he wouldn't wake anyone up with the noise of the car engine starting.

He certainly was a sly one, was Sly Dog.

Watch Dog and Hero both leapt forward to catch Sly Dog before he could push the car any further.

But they didn't leap very far.

WHUMP! WHUMP!

Hero and Watch Dog both fell flat on their faces.

Bossy had tripped them over.

By the time they had picked themselves up, Sly Dog had jumped into the moving sports car—let it roll just a little further downhill—and then had started up the engine and was well away along the road.

"What on earth did you do that for?"

gasped Hero, brushing the dirt from his jumper.

"So that you couldn't stop Sly Dog from getting away in the car," grinned Bossy, racing towards her Daddy's old van, parked at the side of the road. "Now we have *got* to chase Sly Dog in Daddy's van, and we shall really find out what he is up to."

Hero looked at the sports car disappearing up the road and knew that they must get after it straight away or it would soon be out of sight.

"In you get, Watch Dog," he gasped, pushing Watch Dog into the driver's seat of Daddy's van. "Now put your foot down and drive as fast as you have ever driven in your life."

"That's the stuff!" grinned Bossy. "You really sound like a Hero when you talk like that, Hero."

Then Bossy stopped speaking for suddenly Police Dog Dependable plodded round the corner.

"Hallo, what's this, then?" he wanted to know.

"Ahem," coughed Bossy, thinking quickly for Police Dog Dependable had taken out his notebook and was starting to make notes. "Watch Dog is taking me and my brother for a little moonlight drive." Then *"Get going, Watch Dog,"* she hissed and Watch Dog started the car and drove off before Police Dog Dependable could say another word.

Police Dog shrugged his shoulders.

"Oh well, it's pretty late," said he, "but some people **like** going for moonlight drives."

Then he went on his way.

Meanwhile, along through the streets of Dogsville drove Sly Dog, screeching round the corners and roaring along the straight bits of road.

Bossy nudged Watch Dog in the ribs.

"Faster!" she cried. "Drive faster!"

Watch Dog put his foot down hard against the boards, and the old van nearly took off into the air as it hit a bump.

"I'm going as fast as I can!" he retorted.

Faster and faster he went, until he got out of town and turned the car along the coast road towards Mutville, a very smart town quite a long way away.

And everywhere that Sly Dog drove, Watch Dog and Bossy and Hero rattled along behind in Daddy's old van.

Of course they couldn't keep up—because the sports car had such a powerful engine, but they drove just as fast as they could.

Up hill and down dale they went—across shallow streams, through farmyards—always catching glimpses of Sly Dog in the red sports car as he went over hilltops miles ahead of them.

At last Bossy said: "Well he *must* be going to Mutville—there is nowhere *else* along this road now."

Hero sighed.

"But he will get to Mutville before we can *ever* catch him up," he said. "So how will we ever find out what he does there?"

Bossy glared at Hero.

"Just as we were enjoying a fine adventure, you have to spoil it by asking a sensible question like that," she snapped.

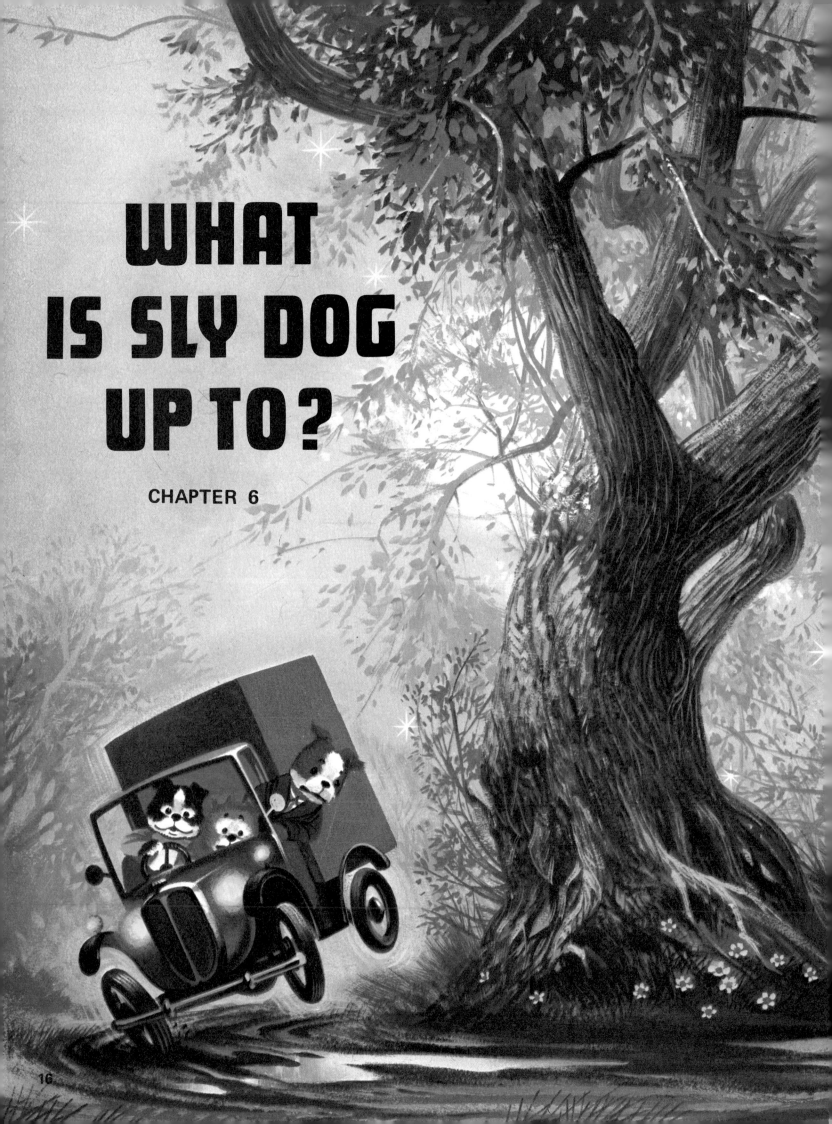

WHAT IS SLY DOG UP TO?

CHAPTER 6

It was half past four in the morning and a beautiful dawn was rising over the hills. Watch Dog was scorching along the country lanes, just as fast as he could go in Daddy Dog's old van.

"Faster! Faster!" shouted Bossy Dog, peering at the road ahead "Sly Dog is miles in front and we shall never catch him at this rate."

Hero sat in the front of the van, clutching his tummy.

"Please don't go any faster, Watch Dog," said Hero "Screeching round all these corners is making me sea-sick." Bossy sniffed in disgust.

"A fine hero you are I must say," she sneered. "Fancy being called Hero and getting a pain in your tummy every time anything exciting happens."

But before Hero could say anything in reply, Watch Dog pushed his foot hard down on the brake pedal and made it stop very quickly. Then he backed it swiftly into a field.

He switched off the engine and hissed:

"Be quiet and watch the road."

The three dogs glued their eyes on the road and in a few minutes they saw their brother Gay Dog's beautiful red sports car speeding back towards them from Mutville.

The car drew level with them and whizzed past—but not so fast that they couldn't clearly see Sly Dog sitting hunched forward over the wheel.

"Well," said Watch Dog, "whatever it was that Sly Dog wanted to do in Mutville, he has done it and he is on his way home again now. So we might as well go, too."

And Watch Dog drove Daddy Dog's old van out of the field and tootled along back towards Bossy's and Hero's home.

They got back to a lovely smell of bacon and eggs and fried tomatoes coming from the kitchen and to see Gay Dog standing outside the garage glaring at his car.

"So Sly Dog brought the car *back* after using it to drive to Mutville then," said Hero, as they drove up 'He didn't steal it for good. Isn't that a funny thing!"

"*You* may think it's funny, but I'm sure Gay Dog doesn't," whispered Bossy. "I'm going to leave you to explain to Gay Dog how his precious car is all smothered with mud. I'm going to help Mummy get the breakfast."

Hero squared his shoulders, got out of the van, and opened his mouth.

"Oh, don't waste your breath trying to explain," snapped Gay Dog, "I can see that my car has got muddy for the third night running, so this time I am really going to call in the police."

So all the Dog Family sat round having breakfast and Police Dog Dependable came in to listen to their story.

"Now let me make sure I have everything straight," he said.

"Well you ought to have," piped up Bossy, as she ate her second slice of toast with extra strawberry jam on it. "We've told you what happened three times. You would have to be pretty thick not to have understood it by now."

Police Dog Dependable gave her a cold stare.

"It isn't that *I* am slow at *understanding*," he said. "It means that certain people, mentioning no names of course, are so busy stuffing themselves with toast and strawberry jam, that they do not tell their stories right in the first place."

"Ha! Ha! Ha! OUCH!"

Hero started to laugh and then squealed as Bossy kicked him under the table.

She would have preferred to have kicked Police Dog Dependable, but of course, she didn't dare.

CHAPTER 7

DOG TIRED and the Bank Robbery

Police Dog Dependable licked his pencil and looked at his notebook.

"Now is this the right story then?" he asked. "Gay Dog, you bought a new sports car."

Gay Dog nodded.

"For two nights running you locked it up in your father's garage and although the car was clean, when you put it away, in the morning, when you got it out, it was covered with mud."

Gay Dog nodded again.

Next, Police Dog Dependable looked at Watch Dog and Bossy, the little girl dog, and her brother Hero, the middle brother in the Dog family.

"Then on the third night you three saw Sly Dog take the car from the garage and drive off in it. You followed in Daddy Dog's old van."

Watch Dog, Bossy and Hero all nodded

"Sly Dog was able to drive so fast in Gay Dog's lovely new car that you couldn't keep up with him. You are as sure as you can be that Sly Dog drove like the wind to Mutville and then drove back here again, and just left Gay Dog's car in the garage where he found it."

Police Dog thought for a moment.

"Well," he said, "of course I could just go and arrest Sly Dog and charge him with taking Gay Dog's car without Gay Dog's permission—but I would rather hang on a bit and find out just *why* he is taking the car."

So Police Dog Dependable phoned the police station in Mutville to ask if anything out of the ordinary had happened in Mutville during the night.

"Anything—yawn—out of the—yawn—ordinary?" answered Sergeant Dog Tired, who was always on night duty. "You must be—yawn—joking. This is the most—yawn—ordinary town that ever was. *Nothing* ever happens here. Not even any-thing *ordinary*—let alone anything *out* of the ordinary—yawn."

And Dog Tired was just about to put the telephone back on its holder and snuggle down for a comfy snooze, when the door of the Mutville Police Station burst open and in ran the manager of the Mutville bank.

"What *do* you think has happened?" panted the bank manager.

Dog Tired pushed up his eyelids to stop himself from dozing off.

Then he spoke into the telephone to Police Dog Dependable.

"Just hold on a minute, would you, please," he said, "I think it's going to be one of those mornings."

Then Dog Tired looked back at the bank manager.

"Well, tell me what has happened then," he said. "The sooner you tell me, the sooner I can get back to sleep again."

"Oh, this is no time for sleeping!" gasped the bank manager. "During the night, someone broke into my bank!"

Dog Tired picked up the phone again.

"Are you still there, Police Dog Dependable?" he asked.

And when Police Dog said "Yes," Dog Tired told him about the bank break-in.

"I shall have to go down to the bank to find out all about things," went on Dog Tired. "As soon as I get back I will ring you up again, Police Dog Dependable."

And hanging up the phone, Dog Tired splashed his face with cold water to wake himself up and hurried down to the Mut-ville Bank with the bank manager.

Meanwhile, back in the Dog Family's home there was a lot of excitement when Police Dog Dependable told them about the bank raid in Mutville.

"That's it, then," said Bossy. "Sly Dog used Gay Dog's car to drive to Mutville to rob the bank. If anyone saw the car and took its number or anything, they would think it was Gay Dog doing the robbery "

"Well, I think Miss Bossy is just about right," said Police Dog Dependable. "I reckon that if I go down to search Sly Dog's house I shall find it full of money missing from the bank."

And Police Dog Dependable was just about to set off for Sly Dog's home, when the phone rang again.

"That will be Dog Tired ringing back," said Daddy Dog.

Police Dog Dependable picked up the phone and heard a great big yawn coming from the other end.

"Yes, it's Dog Tired," he smiled. "Tell me, Dog Tired, how much money was stolen?"

Dog Tired yawned again.

"I told you nothing ever happened in Mutville," he said. "Even when someone breaks into the bank, nothing happens."

"What do you mean?" gasped Police Dog Dependable in surprise.

"Well, someone broke into the bank all right," yawned Dog Tired. "The locks are broken and the doors forced open—but there is no money missing at all!"

CHAPTER 8

BOSSY FINDS OUT FOR HERSELF

My goodness there was a lot of chatting going on in the home of the Dog Family.

Husky Dog, who happened to be pushing a wheelbarrow past the house, stopped to listen. His wheelbarrow was full of medicine bottles, cough drops, gargle mixtures and warm woolly scarves. You see, Husky Dog was always making out that he had a sore throat and he had just been shopping.

He shrugged his shoulders as he heard Bossy's loud voice.

"That sounds like trouble," he croaked. "I'm off," and away he went. Behind him, the Dog Family went on chattering.

They were all talking about how Sly Dog kept stealing Gay Dog's new sports car out of the garage at night—driving it like mad to Mutville and getting it all muddy and then just putting it back in the garage.

And now someone had broken into the bank at Mutville but nothing had been stolen.

"I think I ought to go and see Sly Dog and tell him that if he touches my car again I'll punch him right on the nose," said Gay Dog.

"Oh, trust you to do a stupid thing like that and spoil all the fun!" snapped Bossy, Gay Dog's little sister.

"Fun!" gasped Gay Dog. "What's funny about having my car stolen every night?"

Just at that moment Police Dog Dependable rang the front door bell of the Dog Family's home.

"Good morning!" he said, as Mummy Dog opened the door. "May I speak to Gay Dog, please?"

And Police Dog Dependable came in and explained his plan.

He wanted Gay Dog to leave his car in the garage as usual and let Sly Dog steal it just one more time.

"We know Sly Dog drives your car to Mutville," said Police Dog Dependable, "and although we haven't a car fast enough to keep up with your car, I have arranged with Dog Tired, the police sergeant in Mutville, that he and I will be waiting in a police car in Mutville. We shall follow Sly Dog at the end of his trip and see exactly where he goes and what he does."

"What a super plan!" gasped Bossy, her eyes shining. "Can I come with you?"

Police Dog Dependable smiled in a superior way. "This is police work, dear," he said. "Little girls should stay at home and help their mummies with the washing up."

"Oh, should they!" said Bossy, feeling terribly disappointed and almost like crying. Being Bossy, she didn't cry she kicked her brother, Mummy's Little Diddums instead.

"Ouch!" gasped Mummy's Little Diddums.

That night Gay Dog put his car away in the garage as usual and all the Dog Family went to bed as usual.

And Police Dog Dependable drove all the way over to Mutville and sat in a police car with Dog Tired, the Police dog for Mutville, waiting for Sly Dog to arrive in Gay Dog's car.

Did I say all the Dog Family went to bed as usual?

Well then I was wrong.

Bossy Dog didn't go to bed as usual. She only *pretended* to go to bed.

When all the others were asleep and before Sly Dog had time to steal Gay Dog's car, Bossy Dog crept out into the garden, scrambled in through the window of the garage and slipped into the back of Gay Dog's car.

"Now I shall be sure to find out where Sly Dog goes, because *I* shall be going *with* him," grinned Bossy to herself, "and I shall be sure to find out what he does, because I will peep out of the back of the car and watch him."

Bossy cuddled down in the back of the car feeling very smug.

And sure enough, when it was really dark, the garage door was pushed sneakily open. Glancing stealthily from side to side with his narrow slinky eyes—in came Sly Dog.

He crept into the front seat of the car, released the brake and let the car run out into the road.

Down the hill rolled the car—and then when it was out of sound of the Dog Family's home, Sly Dog started the engine and roared off towards Mutville.

Up hill, down dale, across muddy streams, Bossy had never gone so fast in a car before in her life.

On they roared—and then, to Bossy's surprise, about a mile before Mutville, Sly Dog screeched the car to a halt in front of a little cottage.

Bossy peeped over the side of the car and saw Sly Dog talking to a dog, who had what looked like green printing ink smudged all over his paws and face.

"What a dirty looking dog!" thought Bossy.

Then she gasped: "Why of *course*—that must be *Dirty* Dog—Sly Dog's cousin! I've heard people talking about him."

The two dogs talked for a moment in the cottage doorway.

Dirty Dog showed Sly Dog lots of packets of money, put them in a sack and gave it to Sly Dog.

Then Sly Dog dashed back into the car and drove faster than ever into Mutville.

He flashed past the police car, and at last parked in a small road at the side of the Mutville bank. Taking up the sack, he started to break open the side door of the bank.

"How strange!" gasped Bossy, "He looks as if he is taking a sack of money *into* the bank! But he *can't* be!"

CHAPTER 9

POLICE DOG CAPTURES SLY DOG

Bossy was amazed. There, before her very eyes, Sly Dog was carrying the sack of money *into* the Mutville bank!

"This is ridiculous!" gasped Bossy "Sly Dog is a naughty dog who steals things, so why is he breaking into a bank in the middle of the night and putting money *into* it?"

Now, of course, Bossy knew that the only way to find out was to creep into the bank after Sly Dog and watch and see what he was doing.

But somehow, when Bossy looked up and down the empty street and then at the big black open doorway through which Sly Dog had gone, she didn't feel like following him.

"I wish one of my brothers—even Little Diddums—were here with me," Bossy thought to herself, "then we could go into the bank together and it wouldn't all seem so scary!"

It was lucky for Bossy that just at that moment, who should come creeping up the road but Police Dog Dependable and Police Sergeant Dog Tired.

Dog Tired was always on night duty and somehow in the daytime, he never seemed to catch up on his proper sleep.

"Yaaaaaaawn!" mumbled Dog Tired. staring at the muddy sports car standing at the side of the Mutville Bank. "That's the car all right," he went on. Then he looked across at the open side door of the bank.

"And Sly Dog must have gone in through that door to rob the bank." he said. "I tell you what, Police Dog Dependable, I'll have a little snooze in the back of the car here—and then when Sly Dog comes out with the money, we'll catch him."

And Dog Tired started to climb into the back of Gay Dog's car—which was the

one Sly Dog had stolen to drive to the bank in.

But, of course, Bossy was already in the back of the car.

"Look out where you're stepping with your great big feet," snapped Bossy.

The two police dogs started back in amazement.

"Miss Bossy! What are you doing here?" gasped Police Dog Dependable.

"I'm keeping an eye on Sly Dog!" said Bossy. "And I bet I can tell you more about what he has been doing than either of you two have found out!"

And Bossy started telling the police dogs how she had hidden in the back of the car while Sly Dog stole it, how she watched from the back seat while Sly Dog drove like mad almost to Mutville and how he had stopped and taken a sack of money from Dirty Dog.

But the strange thing was that Police Dog Dependable didn't seem to want to listen—he seemed more interested in keeping Bossy quiet.

"Very interesting—but keep your voice down" Police Dog Dependable kept muttering.

"It's my duty to tell you everything I have seen," Bossy said, rather angrily. "Sly Dog drove to this bank and took the sack of money and went *into* the bank."

"Miss Bossy—please be QUIET!" cried Police Dog Dependable, getting so upset that in the end, he was making just as much noise as Bossy was himself.

"I won't be quiet," shouted Bossy "You're just jealous because I have found out more than you have."

"Miss Bossy—if you won't be quiet I shall have to put my hanky over your mouth," growled Police Dog Dependable "OOOOOUUUUUCH!"

How Police Dog Dependable squealed, as Bossy nipped him in the hand with her sharp little teeth.

"You lay one paw on me and I will tell my Mum of you!" she yapped.

"What I am trying to tell you," growled Police Dog Dependable, "is that if you go on making all this noise, Sly Dog will hear us and run away!"

Suddenly Bossy was silent, and in the sudden silence, Police Dog Dependable pricked up his ears.

From the front of the bank he heard the sound of running feet.

Bossy and Police Dog Dependable raced round to the front of the bank and there—dashing up the road—was Sly Dog, with a sack of money over his shoulder.

"After him!" gasped Bossy.

And she and Police Dog Dependable pelted up the road after Sly Dog.

Little Bossy ran extra fast, took a flying leap and grabbed Sly Dog by the legs.

Down he went and next moment Police Dog Dependable was sitting on his back.

"I should like you to come to the station with me to answer a few questions," said Police Dog Dependable.

But Bossy was looking at the sack of money in a puzzled way.

"This is the same sack of money that I saw Sly Dog take into the bank!" she said. "Has he robbed the bank — or hasn't he? I'd give a lot to find out!"

CHAPTER 10

SLY DOG'S SLY TRICK

It was dawn in the police station at Mutville. Police Dog Dependable, Police Sergeant Dog Tired, Bossy Dog and the manager of the Mutville bank were all sitting looking at Sly Dog.

Sly Dog was sitting looking very smug and as if he hadn't a care in the world. In front of all of them was the sack full of money.

"Now, look here, Sly Dog, my lad," said Police Dog Dependable. "You have been stealing Gay Dog's car. You have been seen driving it to Mutville. You have been seen breaking into the Mutville Bank. You have been seen running away from the Mutville Bank with a sackful of money. Now, what have you got to say about that?"

Sly Dog sneered. "You've left something out, haven't you?" he laughed and looked at Bossy.

"This young clever-socks here, saw me taking a sack of money *into* the bank — and what's more she has *told you* that she saw me carrying a sack of money into the bank."

Now everyone knew that what Sly Dog said was true—he *had* taken a sack of money *out* of the bank—but then he had taken a sack of money *in* there as well.

Next everyone turned and looked at the bank manager.

"Did you do as I asked and count the

money in the bank on your way here?'' asked Police Dog Dependable.

"Yes, I did,'' said the manager. "And nothing is missing. There is exactly the right amount of money in the bank.''

Sly Dog grinned all across his sneaky face. "So I haven't stolen any money at all, have I?'' he sneered. "All I've done is take a little stroll in and out of the bank in the early morning—and that's not so terrible, is it?''

A silence fell over the police station. The police and Bossy were sure that Sly Dog had been up to no good, but they couldn't see just what he had done wrong.

"Oh, well—'' sighed Police Sergeant Dog Tired, curling up on one of the bunks, "I said nothing ever happened in Mutville. Perhaps all you others will now believe me and go home and let me get some sleep.''

Sly Dog jumped to his feet and picked up the sack of money.

"Only too happy to oblige,'' he smiled.

With glum faces all the others watched him go.

Then Bossy sniffed the air and said, "I say, there is a funny smell where that sack has been.''

She sniffed again.

"It's just like the smell of the morning papers when they first come in through the front door.''

"Oh, you mean the smell of printing ink?'' said Police Dog Dependable then he suddenly gasped, "PRINTING INK! Why, of COURSE!''

Bossy and the bank manager stared at Police Dog Dependable as he smacked one paw into the other. "I see how it was done now!'' he grinned and turned to Bossy.

"You did say that on the way to Mutville, Sly Dog stopped at Dirty Dog's and that was where he picked up the sack of money?''

Bossy nodded.

"While the money was being handed over, did you notice the smell of printing ink then?''

Bossy thought.

"Why, yes I did!'' she gasped. "The smell was quite strong, too.''

Police Dog Dependable smiled. "If we nip over to Dirty Dog's pretty smartly I think we shall find something very interesting,'' he said.

So into the police car jumped Bossy and Police Dog Dependable and the bank manager.

The sky was beautiful with the dawn light as the car squealed to a stop outside Dirty Dog's grubby little shack.

"Open in the name of the law,'' said Police Dog Dependable, hammering on the door. But no one answered.

Police Dog Dependable pushed at the door with his shoulder and burst in—and there inside the shack was a small printing press. And can you guess what it had been printing?

POUND NOTES!

"What a clever plan!'' puffed Police Dog Dependable.

"But if they could print all the pound notes they needed—why bother to break into the bank at all?'' asked Bossy.

★★★★★

GAY DOG'S RIDDLES

Here are some of jolly Gay Dog's riddles for you to solve. See how many you can guess and then test your friends.

1. When you look around on a winter's morning, what do you see on every hand?
2. What always has ten letters in it and may have tens of thousands of letters?
3. When do elephants have eight feet?
4. I am something that can run but can't walk. What am I?
5. What has a hand but can't scratch itself?

ANSWERS
1. Gloves; 2. A post office; 3. When there are two of them; 4. Water; 5. The hand of a clock.

★★★★★

"Because forged pound notes never look quite like the real ones—and if you keep spending them, you are always found out in the end,'' explained Police Dog Dependable. "So Sly Dog obviously had the idea of going into the bank and putting forged pound notes in the place of real pound notes and stealing the real ones. That way he could spend the real money in safety.''

"Well, fancy that! This has probably been going on for days!'' exclaimed the bank manager.

"And now we know why Sly Dog kept taking Gay Dog's car,'' went on Police Dog Dependable. "It's the fastest in town, so Sly Dog could drive in it from Dogsville to Mutville, do his dirty work and be back home again in a very short time.''

"My word, that was clever!'' said Bossy.

So Bossy and Police Dog Dependable went back to Dogsville and Sly Dog and Dirty Dog were taken to the police station.

Gay Dog got his car back—and it was never stolen again.

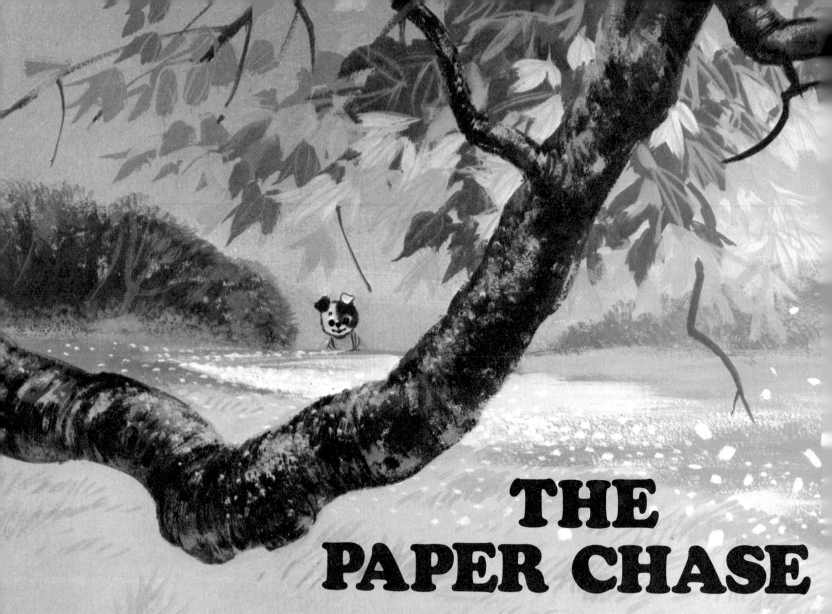

THE PAPER CHASE

Now in the evening, if the children had been good — or if Daddy Dog was in a good mood, or if the television had gone wrong and everyone started arguing because they had nothing else to do, Daddy Dog would say, "Come along everyone. Sit quietly and I will read to you."

Well, the dog children loved being read to — I expect you do too, don't you?

So they would sit quietly and Daddy Dog would read.

Well, this evening he was reading a book called Dog Brown's Schooldays — and it just so happened that he read the bit about the boys going on an exciting paper chase.

Two of the boys took a large sack full of torn-up pieces of paper.

They set off a few minutes ahead of the others and scattered a trail of paper wherever they went.

Then all the other boys had to follow the paper trail and try to catch up with the first two boys or follow them to where the trail ended.

It all sounded great fun and the next day Bossy, the little girl dog, said to her baby brother, Mummy's Little Diddums: "Shall we play at paper chases today?"

Diddums thought it would be a wonderful idea.

"We will tear up lots of newspaper," said Bossy, "put it in that old school satchel hanging up in the hall cupboard and then I will set off running and five minutes after I have gone, you can start after me."

"Lovely!" said Diddums. "Let us start tearing up the paper straight away."

Well, as I expect you will agree, tearing up paper is fun, so the little dogs were sitting down enjoying themselves, before they even started on the actual paper chase.

But then Mummy came into the room.

"I hope that isn't today's paper you are tearing up," she said.

Bossy smiled in a very superior way.

"Of course not," she smiled. "I'm not stupid. This is Friday's paper and today is Monday, isn't it?"

"Yes," said Mummy, "but then she looked at the paper in a worried way, "but that isn't one of the daily papers, is it — it is the **weekly** paper the one that tells us all about what films are on at the cinema and who wants to sell second hand cars and houses and things like that — and the one that comes out on Fridays is the one that has to last all the week."

"Oh dear!" gasped Bossy. "Will Daddy be cross?"

Mummy looked at the torn up bits of paper, "Well, luckily you haven't torn up the bits of the paper that Daddy likes to read," she smiled, "but be more careful in future and ask me before you start to tear anything up."

So then Mummy gave the little dogs some newspaper that really was old and then they went on with their tearing.

"That was a narrow squeak," gasped Mummy's Little Diddums. "In the story in the book, they didn't say you might get into trouble for tearing up the wrong paper!"

But on they went with their game and soon Bossy was ready to go.

She slung the satchel full of torn-up newspaper over her shoulder and padded through the front gate.

Down the road she ran, flinging handfuls of torn-up paper over her shoulder as she went.

What fun it all was.

"I will throw plenty of paper so that the trail is easy for Little Diddums to follow," smiled Bossy, who was in a good mood that morning.

But then at the bottom of the hill, who should come cycling along but Police Dog Dependable.

"Hallo, Police Dog," smiled Bossy, as she skipped along. "Lovely day, isn't it!"

"Well, yes, Bossy, it is a **nice** day, but it isn't turning out to be a very **tidy one**, is it?" said Police Dog, stopping his cycle right in front of Bossy, so that she had to stop running.

"What do you mean?" asked Bossy.

"Well you are making a fine mess with all that paper you are throwing about," said Police Dog Dependable "And just between you and me, I think you ought to stop it."

Bossy glanced back at all the trail of newspaper lying across the pavement.

"Oh, that's all right," she smiled. "I'm not making a mess. I'm making a paper trail for a paper chase."

"Well, you could have fooled me," said Police Dog Dependable, looking rather stern.

"Really it's all right," said Bossy, "we are only doing what the boys did in Dog Brown's Schooldays."

"Well, laying paper trails might have been all right in Dog Brown's days," said Police Dog, "but it isn't good enough here and now, I can tell you."

Just then Little Diddums came along.

"You left a super trail, Bossy," he puffed, "I followed it with no trouble at all."

"Good!" smiled Police Dog Dependable. "Then you can both clear it up with no trouble at all and don't let me see you throwing paper about the streets like that again."

The two dogs felt quite glum, as they cleared up all the paper.

"Paper chasing isn't nearly so much fun as it sounds, is it?" sighed Diddums.

But then Bossy had an idea.

"I know," she said, "let's have a chase — but not a **paper one**."

Diddums looked at her.

"We will lay a trail with that wild bird seed that Mummy puts out for the birds in the garden in winter," said Bossy. "The bird-seed won't look messy and in a few hours the birds will eat it up, anyway."

Wasn't that a good idea?

So Bossy laid a trail of bird-seed — and Diddums had fun following it.

It led all the way round the roads back to their own home and after the chase was over Diddums and Bossy, sat on a tree branch, eating cake and watching the birds pecking up the bird-seed trail.

A party for Dog Rose

It was Saturday morning in the home of the dog family.

Gay Dog, Bossy and Little Diddums were all in the kitchen eating breakfast when Bossy reached for one of the pieces of toast Gay Dog had made.

"Shut that door," she said to Diddums. "I'm sitting in a draught."

But when Diddums jumped up to shut the door that led from the kitchen into the hallway, Gay Dog jumped up, too.

"Don't shut that door. Leave it open!" he said.

Bossy stared in amazement.

"But you are always the one who complains about the way we little ones leave doors open," she said. "Why do you suddenly want the kitchen door open?"

But Gay Dog didn't reply.

Now he was looking out of the kitchen window at the postman who was trotting up the garden path with a sack over his shoulder and some letters in his hand.

Then Gay Dog turned to stare at the front door to see the letters plop through the letter box.

"So that's it!" said Bossy. "You wanted the kitchen door left open, so that you could see when the letters came in through the front door. You are waiting for a special letter."

But Gay Dog didn't reply.

He didn't even hear what Bossy was saying.

He was waiting with his breath held to see what letters plopped in through the front door.

Plop! Plop! Plop!

Three letters came in through the door and one was in a *rose pink envelope*.

Gay Dog took one look and jumped for joy.

"YIPEEE! It's come!" he laughed.

He seemed to have forgotten all about the draught.

Gay Dog rushed forward, picked up the

pink envelope, tore it open and took out a card with a beautiful rose drawn in the corner.

"Do you know what this is?" he beamed at Bossy and Diddums.

"Not until you tell us, stupid, of course not," snapped Bossy, who was beginning to feel rather jealous.

Luckily Gay Dog was so happy, he didn't care about being called stupid.

"This," he said, waving the pretty card in the air, "is an invitation to the best, the most super, the most wonderful, the most gorgeous, the most yummy party of the whole year — THIS is an invitation to the coming of age birthday party of DOG ROSE, the beautiful daughter of Sir Top Dog, who lives in the magnificent manor house in the park."

"Really!" said Bossy, who couldn't help feeling impressed. "Well, write straight back and say that we can come. I don't want to miss anything good like that."

Gay Dog rocked with laughter.

"We?" he said "WE? You must be joking. This party is for grown-up young dogs, not little tiddlers like you. Ha! Ha! Ha!"

Bossy was too upset even to say anything rude — which was very unusual for her.

Diddums felt rather sad, because the party sounded so marvellous.

"Still," he said, "Dog Rose is a lot older than we are, Bossy, so it is only natural that she only wants chums of her own age at her party."

But as the day of the party drew nearer and Bossy heard how Sir Top Dog was giving Dog Rose a rose-coloured Mini car for her birthday and how the manor house was going to be decorated with roses in every room, she felt very left out.

The afternoon of the party came and the three young dogs watched their big brother Gay Dog putting on a new suit and a new rose coloured shirt and a rose in his button hole, ready for the party.

Then they saw him wrap up a beautiful rose brooch to take as a present — and off he went.

"I wish we were old enough to go," thought Bossy and Diddums and Hero.

But then driving up to the gate came Sir Top Dog's big car and out of it stepped Sir Top Dog's chauffeur and he was carrying one huge hamper and three parcels.

Bossy and Diddums and Hero began to feel excited. Was there going to be a treat for them after all?

The chauffeur spoke to Mummy Dog and then bent down to the three little dogs.

"Sir Top Dog says he is sorry you are too young to come to the party," smiled the chauffeur, "but to make you happy he has sent you these presents."

And first he gave the children a hamper full of lovely food and then he gave Bossy a parcel with a party dress patterned with rose buds in it. And the boys each had parcels with party shirts in them.

How pleased they all were. Now they could have their own party.

They sat eating the food from the hamper happily all evening.

"Good old Sir Top Dog," smiled Bossy. "And good old Dog Rose, too."

CHAPTER 1

ENTER SEA DOG

The only thing was, Hero wasn't quite grown up yet, and although one half of him was always trying to be a hero, the other half was still a little dog, who thought he ought to be doing what Mummy Dog said.

Well, one day, Hero and his sister, Bossy, had gone down to help their Daddy in his dog biscuit shop.

You remember Bossy, don't you? She is the girl of the family, who likes bossing everyone else about. Do you know anyone like that?

Anyway, half way through the morning, Daddy Dog said, "Do you think you two could look after the shop on your own for half an hour while I go out in the van to deliver some biscuits to Sir Top Dog?"

"I'll do my very best, Daddy," Hero started to say, when he was, of course, interrupted by Bossy.

"Of course we can look after the shop," she beamed. "At least I can. I'm good at everything."

Bossy had a very big opinion of herself.

Well, as it happened, Daddy hadn't been gone long, when who should come breezing into the shop but Sea Dog.

Now, Sea Dog could tell some very interesting stories, but he was also very tough. Very tough indeed.

Hero looked at Sea Dog's weatherbeaten face and the red spotted scarf knotted round his head and the golden ear-rings in his ears and the cutlass hanging from his waist and the pistol tucked in his belt, and decided it was time to be polite.

"Good morning, sir," smiled Hero, "What can I do for you?"

"Well, sonny, to start with you can fetch your father," growled Sea Dog. "I don't have any truck with whipper-snappers like you."

"What a cheek!" gasped Bossy. "You aren't going to let him speak to you like that, are you, Hero? Go round to the front of the counter and kick him!"

But Hero waved Bossy back.

"Sea Dog is a customer and I must always be polite to customers," he said.

Then he turned to Sea Dog.

"I'm afraid my father is out for about half an hour, but I can serve you with biscuits, if you like," he said.

Sea Dog suddenly looked very crafty.

"So your dad won't be back for half an hour, will he?" grinned Sea Dog in a sneaky sort of way. "In that case, you can serve me with two big sacks of best, long-lasting dog biscuits, and that scruffy little lazybones behind the counter there can help me load them on to my pushcart."

Bossy was speechless with fury at being called a scruffy little lazybones.

And even Hero, who knew he ought to be polite to customers, felt his blood begin to boil a little.

"Mr. Sea Dog, sir," said Hero, "I should certainly appreciate it if you could be a little more polite when you talk about my sister."

"Stop all that fancy talk and go out and kick him," hissed Bossy, but Hero wouldn't listen.

"Now stop all this fussing and sell me these biscuits or, shiver my timbers, I'll go and buy them from another shop," growled Sea Dog.

So Hero struggled out with the big sacks of biscuits and loaded them on to Sea Dog's cart.

Of course, Bossy was too offended to help.

"That will be five pounds, please, Mr. Sea Dog," said Hero at last. "I have given you the very best biscuits."

Sea Dog took out two pound notes and put them on the counter.

"Here you are, sonny," he said. "And think yourself lucky to get it."

"Oh no, sir," said Hero. "You have made a mistake. Those biscuits are worth five pounds."

"The biscuits are worth what you can get for them," said Sea Dog with a horrid sneer. "And all a little half-grown pup like you can get out of a tough old seadog like me is two pounds. You were the one who made a mistake when you told me your Daddy wasn't here. Your Daddy's too big for me to cheat, but you're not."

Suddenly Hero felt all the "being brave" part of him burning up inside him and telling him to snatch the biscuits back or else make Sea Dog hand over the rest of the money.

But then another little voice inside him was saying, "What will Mummy say if you get hurt? You know she doesn't like fighting."

But suddenly Hero heard a yell of rage. Bossy, who never had any little voices arguing inside her, had gone round to the front of the counter and had given Sea Dog a hard kick.

"Hand over the rest of the money or I will kick you again," she yapped.

"Why, you little tyke," yelled Sea Dog.

It was when Hero saw Sea Dog getting ready to give Bossy a good spanking, that he became a real hero.

"Don't you dare lay a finger on my sister!" he shouted, and, leaping over the counter, he banged Sea Dog over the head with a bag of biscuits. Then he snatched away his sword and pistol, tripped him over and sat on his chest. Meanwhile, Bossy tickled Sea Dog's feet, until he was only too eager to hand over the other three pounds and get away.

So everything ended well, but Bossy kept thinking to herself. "I wonder why Sea Dog wanted so many long-lasting dog biscuits? I bet he is going off on an adventure. I will try to find out more about it."

I n these stories, I have told you about Hero, haven't I? He is older than Mummy's Little Diddums and Bossy, but younger than Gay Dog.

He was called Hero because he had been born when the Dog Star was high in the sky, and all dogs born then turn out to be heroes.

CHAPTER 2
BURIED TREASURE

Bossy thought for a long time and then she said over breakfast the next day: "I think there's something fishy about Sea Dog."

"Ha, Ha! Well, there would be, with him spending so much time at sea, wouldn't there?" laughed Little Diddums, who was Bossy's smallest brother.

"Oh, shut up!" snapped Bossy. That is something big sisters often say to little brothers, as you will know if you are a little brother and you have a big sister.

"What I meant was," went on Bossy, "that I think Sea Dog is up to something — and, knowing Sea Dog, the something he is up to is bound to be mysterious and exciting and perhaps bad or wicked or even naughty as well."

By this time everyone sitting round the table was looking at Bossy.

"I think Sea Dog bought all those biscuits because he is going off on a voyage," she said. "Why, I bet he's going off on a pirate raid. In a few days we shall be reading in the papers that ships have been sunk by a mysterious sailing boat flying the Jolly Roger."

At this, of course, everyone started to laugh—everyone except Mummy's Little Diddums, who was asking who Roger was and why he was jolly.

Now Bossy didn't like being laughed at, so she turned and started snapping at poor Little Diddums again.

"The Jolly Roger is the pirate skull-and-crossbones flag," she sneered. "Fancy being so stupid as not to know that."

Diddums might have been upset at all this snapping and sneering, but he had a very nice nature, and said:

"I know you are only sneering at me because you are upset that the others are laughing at you, Bossy, so I forgive you."

"Oh, you're so good-natured you make me sick," snapped Bossy again and stomped up to her room.

Her eldest brother, Gay Dog, was still laughing as he went off to work.

"Fancy Bossy thinking that Sea Dog could go pirate raiding in that little sailing ship of his," he chuckled. "Why, the police would soon be after him."

Daddy Dog nodded.

"Yes," he smiled, "but I shouldn't be surprised if Bossy isn't a little bit right. I don't suppose Sea Dog is off on any pirate raids, but he could still be up to mischief of some sort."

Diddums pricked up his ears when he heard that.

"Bossy would be pleased to know that Daddy thinks she might be right," he smiled—and he raced upstairs at once.

He was so sweet, he couldn't bear to think of Bossy being unhappy, even though she **had** snapped at him.

"Bossy! Bossy!" he called, bouncing into Bossy's room. "I heard Daddy say he thinks you may be right about Sea Dog being up to mischief."

Bossy **was** pleased. She brushed away a little tear she had been shedding all on her own and smiled at Diddums.

"Thanks for coming and telling me," she said. "Sometimes you aren't too bad at all. Will you come with me to spy on Sea Dog and try to find out what he is up to?"

"Well, I'll have to ask Mummy first," said Diddums a little doubtfully. "You know we aren't supposed to go out without telling her."

"Oh, you and your goody-goody ways!" sighed Bossy, but she knew Diddums was right, and down they went to speak to Mummy.

"Mummy," said Diddums, "may we go out to spy on Sea Dog? . . . ouch!"

Bossy gave Diddums a hard dig with her elbow to stop him from saying any more.

"What Diddums meant to say was, may we go out for a walk to get some fresh air, so long as we are careful of the traffic?" said Bossy.

"Well, yes," said Mummy, "you can go out. But don't go too far, don't talk to any strangers, and be home for dinner at one o'clock."

"Yes, Mummy," smiled Bossy, and raced out of the house dragging Diddums behind her.

Down towards the river they raced, to the little quayside, where a few fishing boats were tied up.

And there floating on the water with the other boats was the tough jaunty sailing ship belonging to Sea Dog. Everyone agreed it was a spanking fine little craft and it was called the Merry Mermaid— and had a wooden figure of a mermaid carved on the bows.

As they drew near the Merry Mermaid, Bossy and Diddums walked very quietly so that Sea Dog couldn't hear them coming.

Sea Dog was sitting on the deck in the sunshine, looking at a piece of paper.

Bossy and Diddums crept close enough to look down on to Sea Dog and the paper. It was a map.

At the top of the map was written BURIED TREASURE.

Bossy gasped and clutched at Diddums in her excitement.

"I knew it!" she said.

CHAPTER 3

Who can stay up all night?

The sound of Bossy's voice made Sea Dog look up.

He wasn't at all pleased to see the two youngsters peering down at him.

"Be off with you," he shouted, turning the map over so that they couldn't see it any more. "Be off with you, or I'll have you swabbing the decks and mending the sails before you've got time to say 'Ship ahoy!'"

Bossy didn't wait to say anything.

She just grabbed Diddums by the hand and ran until they were quite out of sight of Sea Dog and his ship, the Merry Mermaid.

"There!" panted Bossy at last. "I was right, after all—did you see?"

"Well, I did see," said Diddums, "but in a way, I didn't."

Bossy stared at him.

"What are you babbling about?" she snapped.

"Well, I saw the map," said Diddums, "but I'm only Mummy's Little Diddums, and I can't read properly yet, and I couldn't read the words at the top."

Bossy sighed.

"It's lucky someone in the family has brains," she replied. "I'm clever enough to read, and those two words at the top of the map said: BURIED TREASURE."

"How clever you are, Bossy!" exclaimed Diddums.

Bossy gave Diddums a smile.

"Sometimes you're quite nice," she said.

"Now," said Bossy, as the two little dogs walked home for their dinner, "it is quite obvious that Sea Dog is stocking up his ship with biscuits so that he can go on a voyage and look for buried treasure."

"We have seen the map and we know he has bought the biscuits," said Diddums.

"There is no doubt about it at all," stated Bossy.

"Yes, I agree with you," said Diddums, "I think you are wonderful the way you work things out."

Bossy smiled at Diddums again. She loved people to tell her how clever she was.

"Sea Dog must be watched all the time to see when he is really ready to sail," she went on. "We must take it in turns to spy on the ship. Perhaps we might even get a chance to photograph the BURIED TREASURE map. We could borrow Gay Dog's camera. I will take the first watch this afternoon—and you can watch during tea time. You don't mind missing tea, do you, Diddums? I can't miss tea, because I get hungry."

Diddums frowned.

"I get hungry, too, you know," he said "I don't want to miss tea, either."

"Oh, you are selfish!" grumbled Bossy. "Fancy fussing because you're going to miss a bit of food!"

"Well, you don't want to miss it, either," began Diddums, and then, because he was so sweet, he went on. "But if someone has to miss tea, I suppose I had better be unselfish and let it be me."

"Good!" said Bossy. "And if you are feeling unselfish, then you can take the night watch as well."

Diddums was shocked.

"What, stay out all night?" he gasped "In the cold and dark without my little teddy bear, bedside light or my hot water bottle?"

"Well, surely you don't expect **me** to do it!" snapped Bossy. "I'm a **girl**."

And sweet Little Diddums was just going to say he would **have** to take the night watch too, when he suddenly remembered something.

"Talking like this is just a waste of time," he said, heaving a sigh of relief. "Mummy would never let us do it anyway."

"She wouldn't want **me** to miss tea, because I know she is making my favourite cake with white icing," Bossy admitted. "And she would never let either of us stay out all night because she never does."

Bossy looked glum.

"Well, we'll just have to do it without telling her, then," she said. "I'm determined to find out what Sea Dog is up to."

Now, Diddums was truthful as well as being sweet-natured.

"I will never do anything naughty like that," he said. "I will never do anything without telling Mummy."

And, of course, Bossy knew Diddums was right.

Then, suddenly, as they were passing a thatch-roofed cottage, with roses and honeysuckle growing in the garden, Diddums heard something that gave him an idea.

Tick-tock, tick-tock, tick-tock, tick-tock!

The sound of dozens of watches ticking came floating over the garden hedge.

"Of course!" smiled Diddums, "WATCH Dog!"

Diddums grabbed Bossy by the arm and laughed.

"All our problems are solved," he said. "Watch Dog is grown up—he can stay out as long and as late as he likes. He's used to staying up all night watching things—that is his job."

The two dogs ran into the garden of Watch Dog's house and there was Watch Dog sitting having a doze in the sunshine.

And, as usual, all up and down his arms were his watches, ticking away.

You see, he was called Watch Dog not only because he earned his living by watching things, but because he just loved watches as well—and he wore lots of them.

That is why Diddums and Bossy had heard so many watches ticking as they walked past the garden.

Watch Dog opened his eyes and smiled at Bossy and Diddums.

"Will you help us find some BURIED TREASURE?" asked Bossy.

Watch Dog opened his eyes even wider.

"Yes, please!" he said.

CHAPTER 4

WATCH DOG Takes A Tumble

Police Dog Dependable looked at what he had written in his notebook. "Now, let's make sure I've got this straight, Miss Bossy," he said. "You say that you know that Sea Dog has been loading up his ship the Merry Mermaid, with dog biscuits and you say that you have seen him looking at a map headed BURIED TREASURE?"

"Yes, and do you remember that years ago everybody thought that Sea Dog had stolen a collection of gold coins from Sir Top Dog's house?" went on Bossy.

Police Dog Dependable looked at Bossy and her family who were just having their dinner.

"I'll have you know, young lady, that the police always remember everything," he said. "Do you think that Sea Dog did steal those gold coins and that he buried them on a secret island? Now, after all these years you think he is going back to dig them up again?"

"Yes, I do!" said Bossy firmly.

Police Dog Dependable thought for several moments. "Well, I think you might be right," he said. "I must certainly look into it all. And the first thing I must do is to go down and see Watch Dog. You say he is watching Sea Dog and the Merry Mermaid for any signs of setting sail?"

"Yes, sir," said Little Diddums. "Watch Dog kindly went to watch Sea Dog so that we could come home to dinner and Mummy wouldn't be cross with us for being late."

Police Dog Dependable sniffed.

"Yes, and a very nice dinner it smells, too. No one should be late for a dinner like that."

Mummy Dog smiled across at Police Dog Dependable.

"Well, all the stew has gone," she said, "but you are welcome to a slice of jam pudding and cream if you like."

Police Dog Dependable looked pleased.

"If you insist. I will have a tiny piece," he smiled.

Dinner was over at last and after thanking Mummy Dog, Police Dog Dependable got on to his bicycle and pedalled off towards the river.

"You youngsters stay at home," he called. "This is police work."

"Police work my foot!" hissed Bossy to Diddums and to her middle brother, Hero, who had been listening to everything over the dinner table. "Police Dog is just trying to keep all the fun for himself. I don't care what he says, let's go down to the river and watch what happens."

"Well, just going down to watch can't hurt, can it?" said Hero to Diddums.

"I suppose not," said Diddums. "But if we all go out, who is going to help Mummy with the washing up?"

You see, only the youngest three dogs were home for dinner at midday.

"Oh, you! Why can't you just come out and leave Mummy to do the washing up without bothering?" snapped Bossy. "Now you're making us all feel bad."

But Little Diddums wouldn't go.

"I will catch up later," he said.

So Bossy and Hero took a short cut across the fields down to the river, and Diddums went into the kitchen to help his mummy with the washing up.

MEANWHILE, down by the river, Sea Dog had been doing some thinking.

Ever since he had looked up and seen Bossy and Diddums looking down into his boat he had been wondering if they had seen his map with the words BURIED TREASURE written across the top.

"I don't want anyone spying round me just at this moment," muttered Sea Dog to himself. "I must be more careful."

So, unluckily, when Watch Dog came strolling along the riverside, Sea Dog was ready for him.

Watch Dog thought he was being very clever. He sat down quite near Sea Dog's ship, the Merry Mermaid, and looked across at an old fishing boat called the Happy Herring.

"Good morning, Sea Dog," smiled Watch Dog. "Old Salty Sam has asked me to keep watch on his boat, the Happy Herring, for him."

Watch Dog knew that in fact Salty Sam was at home with a cold, but Sea Dog wasn't in a very trusting mood. He knew that Watch Dog was a friend of Bossy and Diddums and he guessed at once that Watch Dog was really watching **him**.

"I must get rid of Watch Dog," thought Sea Dog. So he called out:

"I'm very glad you've come along, Watch Dog. I thought I saw someone moving about on the Happy Herring a little while ago. You had better go and have a look."

Well, after saying he was supposed to be watching the Happy Herring, Watch Dog couldn't very well refuse. So he scrambled to his feet and stepped on to the deck of the Happy Herring.

Sea Dog came and stood behind him.

"Look down in the hold," said Sea Dog. "That's where I thought I saw someone moving about."

The hold is the downstairs part of the ship.

Of course, you can guess what happened.

As Watch Dog bent over to look down through the trapdoor leading to the hold, Sea Dog gave him a push.

WHUMP!

Down into the hold fell Watch Dog.

Sea Dog slammed the trapdoor shut and bolted it.

"Now no one will come to let Watch Dog out until tomorrow," he smiled, "so I can get on with my plans in peace."

You see, Sea Dog knew that Salty Sam was home with a cold as well. But, of course, he wasn't going to be left in peace, was he?

Bossy was on his trail.

CHAPTER 5

Where are Bossy and Hero?

BANG! Bang! Bang!
"Help! Help!"
Bangriddy-bang-bang! Bang! Bang!
"Help! Helpity-help!"

All that noise and shouting was being made by Watch Dog, from the hold of the fishing boat, the Happy Herring.

Sea Dog looked across from his own boat, the Merry Mermaid, and frowned.

"I can't have Watch Dog making all that noise," he muttered to himself, "or someone will soon come along to see what is the matter."

And Sea Dog didn't want anyone coming along, because he was up to no good—no good at all.

So then Sea Dog did a very naughty thing.

He trotted up to the good ship Happy Herring, and untied the mooring rope.

At once the Happy Herring started to drift down the river towards the sea, half a mile away.

"Now," grinned Sea Dog nastily, "anyone who comes poking their noses about down here, will chase after the Happy

Herring to rescue Watch Dog. I shall be left to get on with my own affairs in peace.''

Wasn't Sea Dog naughty?

You would never do anything horrid like that, **would** you?

Anyway, as the Happy Herring and all the banging noises and shouts of help drifted further and further away, Sea Dog turned back to his own little boat, the Merry Mermaid.

When he was sure that everything was ready, Sea Dog untied the rope that held his ship to the quayside, and then the Merry Mermaid started to chug-chug away **UP** the river.

That was a surprise, wasn't it?

You were thinking that Sea Dog was going to sail the Merry Mermaid out to sea, weren't you? But he didn't.

He sailed up the river—inland.

ANYWAY, while all this had been going on, Police Dog Dependable had been cycling down to the river.

The little dogs, Bossy and Diddums and Hero, had been telling him all about how they thought Sea Dog was going to dig up some gold coins he had stolen, several years before.

So down to the river went Police Dog Dependable to find out what was going on.

Now, it was lucky that he cycled down to join the riverside tow-path, just a little further towards the sea from the spot where the Merry Mermaid was tied up.

It was lucky for Watch Dog, that is, because as Watch Dog drifted along in the Happy Herring, banging and shouting, he drifted right past Police Dog Dependable.

Police Dog Dependable knew at once that something was wrong.

Police Dog Dependable cycled along the tow path, until he came to a bend in the river, where he knew the Happy Herring would drift close to the bank.

Then, throwing down his cycle, Police Dog Dependable made a huge leap and just managed to cling to the side of the Happy Herring. Then he scrambled aboard.

Wasn't he brave?

It didn't take long to rescue Watch Dog from the hold of the Happy Herring.

And it took even less time for Watch Dog to tell Police Dog how Sea Dog had pushed him into the hold and bolted the trapdoor after him.

But it did take quite a long time to get the engine of the Happy Herring started, to get Police Dog's bicycle aboard, and the little fishing boat turned round and chugging back up the river to where they had last seen the Merry Mermaid.

And of course, when Watch Dog and Police Dog and the Happy Herring did get back to where they had last seen Sea Dog and the Merry Mermaid—they weren't there.

They had gone—gone right away—and there was no sign left of them at all.

THAT'S strange!'' said Watch Dog. ''I wonder where they can be?''

''Well, there's one thing that's sure,'' said Police Dog. ''They can't have gone past us out to sea, or we should have seen them. They must have gone up river.''

Police Dog wrote in his notebook everything that had happened so far, and then he said:

''I can see that it is my duty to go after Sea Dog and find out what mischief he is up to, but'' —here Police Dog looked round at the fishing boat, the Happy Herring, and gave a few sniffs—''but I don't see that it is my duty to chase after him in this smelly old fishing boat. In any case, the Happy Herring doesn't belong to the Police, so I can't really take it. I shall tie it up safely again and ride my bicycle up the tow path and chase Sea Dog that way.''

Well, it all sounded like the right thing to do to Watch Dog.

''I think I will go home and have a bath and wash all this fishy smell off myself and my clothes,'' he said.

''Good idea,'' smiled Police Dog. ''Police work is best left to the police.''

And they were just about to set off on their separate ways, when Diddums came rushing down to the riverside.

''Tell me what's been going on—puff—have I—puff—missed any excitement—puff—and where are Bossy and Hero?'' gasped Diddums.

Police Dog was very surprised to see Diddums.

''I haven't seen Bossy and Hero,'' he said. ''And I told you children to stay at home, anyway.''

''I know!'' sighed Diddums. ''But Bossy and Hero **would** insist on going after you to see what happened. I just stayed to help Mummy with the washing up—and then I came as well. But if you haven't seen Bossy and Hero—what can have happened to them?''

CHAPTER 6

Police Dog on the trail

Well, if you children had done as I told you, we should know where they are," said Police Dog in a rather annoyed voice, "you would all be safe at home, where I told you to stay."

Diddums hung his head.

"I know," he sighed, "but when my sister Bossy gets an idea in her head, it's more than I can do to stop her. She's my Bossy big sister, that's why we call her Bossy, you know ....."

Diddums voice trailed away.

Bossy might be bossy, but Diddums loved her and he was rather worried about her — and his brother Hero, as well.

"You don't suppose Sea Dog has done anything to them, do you?" he whispered.

Watch Dog couldn't help laughing.

"I'd like to see the day when anyone get the better of your sister Bossy," he chuckled, "and in any case that brother of yours, Hero, is a very brave fellow. Don't you worry about those two, Little Diddums."

Diddums looked more hopeful.

Police Dog frowned.

"I wish you two would leave all this to me and stop interfering," he said. "Now, Watch Dog, you run along home and just get on with your own affairs. Diddums — you can go to your Daddy at the Dog Biscuit Shop and ask him to go down to the Police Station and ask my assistant Constable Bloodhound to look for Bossy and Hero — and then you go home and stay home. Do you understand?"

"Yes, sir," said Diddums — and away he and Watch Dog scampered.

Police Dog gave a sigh of relief.

"Now perhaps I can get on with my job," he said.

He climbed on his bicycle and started to pedal up the tow-path.

Police Dog knew that this was the way the Merry Mermaid and Sea Dog must have gone.

"And I'm pretty sure that this is the way that Bossy and Hero have gone too," he thought to himself. "If they were spying on Sea Dog — which I don't doubt they were — when they saw him sailing up the river, they would have followed him."

So on up the tow-path pedalled Police Dog.

And sure enough in just a few yards, he saw two sets of paw-prints — just the right size for Bossy and Hero.

"Yes," he smiled. "They just let Sea Dog get far enough ahead so that he wouldn't notice them and then they ran after him."

"Oh, well," chuckled Police Dog, cycling along faster and faster, "I shall soon catch up with those two. Then I will give them a piece of my mind and send them home. Children should leave this dangerous sort of work to the police."

But Police Dog hadn't gone much further, when he saw that the two sets of paw-prints stopped.

There was a whole circle of little footprints.

Then one set of bicycle tracks went on up the tow-path.

And there was no more sign of the footprints of either Bossy or Hero.

"Aha!" grunted Police Dog. "Something has been going on here."

He stopped cycling and put one foot on the ground and looked round.

There was a little cottage at the side of the river and in the garden was a young dog who was counting several silver and copper coins.

"Hallo there, sonny!" said Police Dog, "have you seen a girl and boy recently?" recently?"

The young dog looked up.

"Oh yes," he said. "They borrowed my bicycle."

Then he went on:

"The girl said she would give me her pocket money, if I would let her borrow the bicycle for the afternoon. Then she said that if I **didn't** let her borrow my bicycle, she would box my ears — so I let her have it."

Police Dog sighed.

"That sounds like Bossy all right," he said. "I am on the right trail."

So on went Police Dog.

Then suddenly — what a surprise he had.

Out of the bushes in front of him sprang — BOSSY!

"SHUSH!" she hissed in a loud whisper.

She pulled Police Dog off his bicycle and down into the bushes, where Hero was already hiding with the little boy's bicycle.

"Don't you — **puff** — tell — **pant** — me to be quiet — **gasp — gasp!**" splattered Police Dog crossly.

"Well, somebody's got to tell you," snapped Bossy. "You're puffing and panting and gasping enough to warn the whole river that you're coming."

She peeped through the bushes.

"And," she added, "Sea Dog and the Merry Mermaid are only just round the corner."

Police Dog leaned forward and peeped through the bushes, too.

Round the corner right out in the middle of the river was an island.

Tied up to the island was the Merry Mermaid.

Standing up on the Merry Mermaid was Sea Dog.

In one of Sea Dog's hands was a shovel.

In the other hand was a map.

"There!" hissed Bossy triumphantly, "just look at that shovel. He's going to dig up the buried treasure. What did I tell you!"

CHAPTER 7

The swim to the island

But Police Dog Dependable was thinking hard.

"What I don't understand," he said "is that if Sea Dog was only coming this little way up the river—why did he get his boat, the Merry Mermaid, ready for a long voyage.

Bossy looked at Police Dog Dependable.

"Well, I can tell you one thing," she said.

Police Dog looked up eagerly.

"What's that then, Miss Bossy?" he asked.

"You'll never find out any of the answers sitting here in the bushes, mumbling to yourself," replied Bossy.

She was very cheeky like that, you know, I hope **you** never speak to grown-ups in that saucy way.

Well, while all this chatting had been going on, Hero had been looking across at the island in the middle of the river.

"I say," he said, "Sea Dog has gone into the centre of the island—and he took the shovel and the map with him. Do you think he has started digging for the treasure?"

The three dogs stood silent and pricked up their ears. Across from the island drifted the thud—flop, thud—flop—of someone digging a shovel into the ground and then throwing a shovel full of earth aside.

Bossy looked at the island.

Because of all the trees and bushes she couldn't see what Sea Dog was doing.

Then Bossy looked at Police Dog Dependable and Hero.

"Well, don't just sit there—do something," she yelped.

Police Dog looked at all the wet water between him and the island.

"I don't fancy a swim at the moment," he said. "It's the wrong time of the year. The best thing for me to do is to go to the nearest telephone and call up the coastguards and get them to come round in one of their boats. They'll stop Sea Dog before he can get very far."

"What?" shrieked Bossy. "Let someone else have all the fun capturing Sea Dog and finding all that treasure—when we've done all the hard work! That may be good enough for you—but it's not good enough for me—not by a long chalk."

And Bossy slipped into the water and

started to swim across to the island.

"I'm going to see what Sea Dog's digging up," she called back over her shoulder. And she was gone.

Hero watched his sister go off. He hadn't wanted to swim across to the island at all. You see, Hero wasn't quite grown up—so sometimes he still felt like a little chap who didn't want to do brave things at all.

"Supposing she gets cramp or something and can't swim all the way to the island!" he thought. "Supposing she does get to the island and Sea Dog sees her—and supposing Sea Dog is in one of his nasty moods—why, then Bossy will need me there to protect her."

And, slithering down to the water's edge, Hero slipped into the water and began to swim across to the island, too.

"Oh, dear! Oh, dear!" sighed Police Dog Dependable. "How easy my job would be if only people would stop interfering."

He started to pull off his helmet and jacket.

"If only those little dogs had stayed at home as I told them, I could have called up the coast-guard, got them round here in a boat, had Sea Dog picked up, everything sorted out and I could have been home to tea with Mrs. Police Dog, all nice and cosy."

He pulled off his heavy trousers, so that he was only wearing his long underwear.

Then he gritted his teeth and slipped into the cold river water.

"Ugh!" he gasped.

The water felt very cold to poor Police Dog Dependable—river water does seem to get colder as you get older, you know.

But he knew it was his duty to follow the children and see that no harm came to them.

And Police Dog Dependable always did his duty.

Across to the island paddled Police Dog Dependable, and crept up the grassy bank to join Bossy and Hero as they peered at Sea Dog through the bushes.

Sure enough, Sea Dog had been digging a hole in the middle of a little grassy

clearing. And as they watched him, he pulled up a little tin box out of the hole.

"There it is!" whispered Bossy, shaking with excitement. "There's the treasure."

Hero looked doubtful.

"It isn't a very big box," he said. "I don't see how there could be much treasure in that."

Bossy scowled at him.

"Spoilsport!" she hissed.

Sea Dog opened the box and turned it upside down. And out on the grass fell —a KEY!

"Hmmm! Very interesting—and just as I thought," muttered Police Dog Dependable to himself.

But Bossy wasn't in a muttering mood. Somehow or other, she had expected to see a hoard of gold coins come pouring out of the little box—and she was furious when only a little key came tumbling out.

Bossy ran into the middle of the clearing.

"SEA DOG—you ROTTEN THING!" she shouted in a rage.

CHAPTER 8

BANK BOX № 42

My goodness me – a few moments later – what a commotion there was going on on that island in the middle of the river. Sea Dog was trying to snatch up his key and escape on his boat, the Merry Mermaid.

Police Dog Dependable was trying to catch Sea Dog.

"I should like you to come to the police station with me and help me with some enquiries," Police Dog Dependable puffed as he raced after Sea Dog.

Bossy, the little girl dog, was just furious with everyone. She had followed Sea Dog to the island, expecting to see him dig up stolen golden coins—and all he had dug up had been a little key.

Sea Dog was furious, because he hadn't

wanted anyone to follow him to the island at all.

"It's all because of you and your nosy ways that everyone has been spying on me," snapped Sea Dog as he dodged between the trees. "Why, if I ever lay my hands on you, young Miss Bossy, I'll give you such a spanking that you'll wish you'd never been born."

At that, Bossy's brother Hero, who was on the island, too, leapt forward.

"Don't you dare say things like that to my sister," he barked, and, running at Sea Dog's legs, he knocked him over.

In a flash, Police Dog Dependable was sitting on Sea Dog's chest. And next moment, Bossy came and snatched up the key out of Sea Dog's paw.

Bossy looked at the key in disgust.

"A fine sort of buried treasure this is," she sniffed. "Where's all that stolen gold? That's what I should like to know."

Sea Dog shut his mouth tightly and didn't say a word.

But Police Dog Dependable took the key from Bossy and turned it over in his hands. Written down one side were the words: "Barking-on-Sea Bank, Box 42".

"Aha!" said Police Dog Dependable. "Just as I thought."

Bossy looked impatient.

"Well, tell us, then—tell us," she said. "What do you think?"

"Barking-on-Sea is about one and a half day's sailing from here, just down the coast," said Police Dog Dependable. "So if all those years ago, it was Sea Dog who stole the gold coins from Sir Top Dog— then it would have taken him just three days to sail to Barking-on-Sea, put the gold coins in a box, ask the bank to look after the box for him until he called for it and then sail back here. And just at that time Sea Dog was away on a three-day trip, wasn't he?"

"Then," went on Police Dog. "Sea Dog had to hide the key of the bank box away somewhere, so he came and buried it on this island, at night probably, when no one was watching. Then he made a map to remind him where the key was buried.

"Now, all these years later, when he thinks we have forgotten about the coins, Sea Dog has loaded up his boat for a trip and he was going to get the gold out of the bank and go for a nice voyage round the world, enjoying himself."

Bossy shuffled her feet and glared at the key. She was beginning to feel cold and shivery after her swim in the river.

"Yes, I expect you're right, Police Dog," she said, "but it's all jolly disappointing, after I thought I was going to see lots of gold coins all over the place."

But by this time Sea Dog had got his breath back.

"Get off my chest, Police Dog," he said "You can't prove anything against me yet. After all, digging up a key from an island isn't against the law."

"No," smiled Police Dog, "but bolting Watch Dog in the hold of the Happy Herring and setting him adrift is. So you just come to the police station with me and

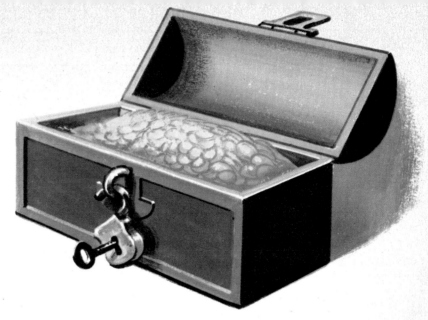

we'll have no more cheeky talk."

So they all clambered into the little ship Merry Mermaid and got safely back to the shore.

Police Dog told his assistant, Constable Bloodhound, not to go looking for Bossy and Hero because they had been found. And everyone went home for tea, warm baths and a cosy evening.

Even naughty Sea Dog was given some of Mrs. Police Dog's home-made chocolate cake and a hot water bottle to keep him comfy in the police cell.

Then, the next morning, when Bossy was feeling good-tempered, Police Dog Dependable came knocking at the door.

"I am going to the bank at Barking-on-Sea to find out what is in box No. 42," he smiled. "As you were such a help in catching Sea Dog, I thought you might like to come, too."

Bossy was thrilled.

"So I shall really see the gold at last!" she gasped.

She looked past Police Dog and saw Sir Top Dog's big car standing at the gate. Sir Top Dog was in the driving seat.

"Sir Top Dog is coming to check that they really are the coins that were stolen from him," explained Police Dog.

So then Bossy, who is really a good sort at heart, said, "Well, as we are going in a big car, do you think my brothers Hero and Little Diddums could come, too?"

Sir Top Dog said yes—so all the little dogs went for the drive to Barking-on-Sea.

They opened the box in the bank—and there were all the gold coins, shining and glimmering just like real treasure.

Bossy and Hero and Little Diddums were thrilled.

Then Sir Top Dog took them all out to a lovely dinner and gave each of the little dogs a gold coin to keep for themselves.

"What a lovely adventure!" sighed Bossy on the way home.

And Mummy's Little Diddums, who has such a kind heart, asked, "Will poor Sea Dog have to spend long in prison?"

"Oh, I don't suppose so," said Police Dog Dependable. "Now that we have got the gold coins safely back again, Old Sea Dog will be out sailing the seas in his little ship the Merry Mermaid again before long."

A SPECIAL CAKE

Diddums," she said. "Nothing would make me wear one of those stupid life jackets. I would never be silly enough to fall over the side. And even if I did, I'm such a good swimmer that it wouldn't matter anyway."

Poor Diddums felt quite upset, but most of all he felt sorry for Bossy.

You see, Diddums knew that Gay Dog made it a rule that he would only take people out with him if they wore life jackets. Now because of all she had said, Bossy would have to choose between looking silly in front of her friends and putting a life jacket on — or not going on the trip at all.

"What can I do?" thought Diddums.

He was very kind hearted and in spite of all the horrid things Bossy had said to him, he was only thinking of helping her.

Diddums felt in his pocket.

Thank goodness — there was a two-penny piece there.

"Just a moment," said Diddums, "I think I have just time to make a phone call before Gay Dog gets back."

Bossy looked puzzled.

Diddums didn't often make phone calls. But then she went back to talking to her friends and took no more notice of Diddums.

So Diddums made his phone call and by the time he got back to the boat, Gay Dog was there, too.

"Well, get your life-jacket on, Bossy," said Gay Dog, "and we will set off."

Bossy grinned.

"I'm not putting one of those baby things on," she laughed, with a glance at her chums to see how grand they thought she was.

Then to Bossy's surprise, Gay Dog put his life jacket on.

"Well, I'm not taking you out unless you **do** put a life jacket on," he said, "so hurry up and make up your mind."

So much for Bossy!

If she put the life jacket on, her friends

One day Gay Dog went out and bought himself a little sailing boat. Then, nearly every week-end Gay Dog went sailing in his boat and it was great fun.

Sometimes he would take his brother Hero with him, because Hero was nearly grown-up and knew how to be quite useful in a boat.

But Gay Dog wasn't very keen on taking his sister Bossy or his youngest brother Diddums with him.

You see they were still quite young and Gay Dog said they were just a nuisance.

But, of course, Bossy and little Diddums **wanted** to go on Gay Dog's boat.

Not really because they liked boating all that much, but just because they wanted to be able to **say** that they had been.

So Mummy Dog kept on at Gay Dog, asking and asking him to take Bossy and Diddums out for a trip.

And in the end, when Mummy promised to knit Gay Dog a lovely sweater, Gay Dog said he would take the two youngsters out.

"But if they start making trouble or being a nuisance — I will bring them straight home again," he said.

Bossy and Diddums were thrilled.

They put on their warm clothes and

then as they stood on the quayside, waiting while Gay Dog went to have a word with the harbour master, Bossy saw that Diddums was putting on a life jacket!

Do **you** know what a life jacket is?

It is a sort of jacket without sleeves that keeps you afloat in the water whether you can swim or not.

Bossy laughed.

She liked laughing at Diddums.

"Cowardy-cowardy-custard! Diddums has to wear a life jacket does he?" she grinned.

Diddums looked surprised.

"Of course!" he said. "Everyone who goes out in little boats is supposed to wear a life jacket — just in case you fall over the side into the water."

"Silly little Diddums is afraid of falling over the side. Ha! Ha!" went on Bossy.

Suddenly she was laughing twice as loud because two of her little girl friends had come along to watch.

"Look at my silly little brother," said Bossy in a loud voice, "he is such a fraidy-puss that he is wearing a life jacket — all because he thinks he is going to be silly enough to fall over the side."

Bossy turned and looked at her friends.

"Well, I'm not a cowardy custard like

would laugh at her.

If she didn't she wouldn't go on the trip.

Gay Dog jumped down on to the deck of his boat and Diddums went with him.

They turned to look at Bossy.

"Are you coming or not?" asked Gay Dog.

"I – er – I ......" Bossy just didn't know what to say.

Then suddenly up rushed Police Dog Dependable with a large cake tin.

"Oh, good! I'm just in time," he puffed.

Diddums looked pleased.

It was Police Dog Dependable he had phoned.

"I want you to try something out for me," said Police Dog, winking at Gay Dog and Diddums, but not letting Bossy or her chums see him wink.

Police Dog held out the cake.

"This is a special cake made by the Sea Dogs Welfare Society," explained Police Dog. "It is specially made to be eaten by sailors when they are wearing life jackets. Two large slices are supposed to be enough to keep you feeling full and warm for an hour. The Sea Dogs Welfare Society want you to try the cake out and tell them if it is all right. But, of course, you can only try it out properly if you are wearing a life jacket," he said, turning to look at Bossy. "Well, Miss Bossy, are you willing to help the Sea Dogs Welfare Society?" he asked.

Bossy said "Yes" at once.

She was very pleased, because now she had a good excuse to put her life jacket on after all, so she would not look silly in front of her friends, but she wouldn't miss her trip either.

"I don't need a life jacket, really," she said, "I am only putting it on to help the Sea Dogs Society."

"Of course," said Police Dog, helping her into the boat.

So Gay Dog and Bossy and Diddums went on their trip and they all wore their life jackets like sensible dogs and they all had some lovely cake.

And they went back and told Police Dog that the cake had kept them full up and warm all the trip.

Diddums and Police Dog grinned at each other, but neither said a word to Bossy.

Afterwards Diddums explained everything to Gay Dog.

"I phoned Police Dog and asked him to bring the cake along and tell us that story just to give Bossy a good excuse to wear her life jacket," said Diddums.

Gay Dog smiled.

"You are a thoughtful little chap," he said.

And he was right.

Sly Dog takes the biscuit

Bossy, the little girl dog, was having a big treat. She was being allowed to help her daddy in his dog biscuit shop.

Bossy loved helping in the shop, because it meant chatting to all the customers and fussing around weighing and wrapping up the biscuits, just like a real grown-up.

But the part she liked best, was at the end of the day, when Daddy shut up the shop and opened the till and counted all the money he had taken that day.

Because, if Bossy had been very good, Daddy would always let her help with counting the money.

And Bossy loved counting money.

Well, that day, Bossy was helping happily in the shop and hoping that Daddy would sell a nice lot of dog biscuits, so that there would be a nice lot of money to count.

"I will put all the notes in one pile and all the silver coins in another pile and all the copper coins in another pile," thought Bossy, "and then I will get out a notebook and pencil and I will write down how many notes we have and how much silver and how much in copper coins."

Then she went on: "And I will add it all up — at least I might let Daddy help me with that — and then we shall know how much money we have made."

It was all going to be great fun, but then half way through the morning, something went wrong.

People stopped coming into the shop.

Bossy stood behind the counter with the biscuits all ready and a big smile on her

THE DOG BISCUIT SHOP IS SHUT— PLEASE BUY YOUR BISCUITS HERE

SLY DOG'S BISCUITS TASTE NASTY

face and her little paw held out ready for the money.

But no one came. No one at all.

"Well, this is a fine thing," thought Bossy. "At this rate, there will be no money for me to count at the end of the day. What is the matter with everybody?"

"Oh, don't worry, Bossy," smiled Daddy. sorting out the new biscuits at the back of the shop. "Someone will be in soon."

But someone wasn't in soon.

Bossy became even crosser.

"I know. The bus bringing people into town must have broken down," muttered Bossy. "It would be just like that stupid bus to break down on the day I am helping in the shop."

But just at that moment, the bus whizzed past the shop window — so Bossy knew there was nothing wrong there.

In the end Bossy decided to go out to see where everyone had got to.

And when she did go out — my, how cross she was. There — on the pavement — just where he couldn't be seen from inside the shop was SLY DOG.

And do you know what the sly thing was doing?

He was standing on the pavement with a huge notice standing beside him.

And do you know what the notice said?

It said:

"The Dog Biscuit Shop is shut — please buy your biscuits here."

And there was a big sack of dog biscuits at Sly Dog's feet.

And what made Bossy jump up and down with rage, was that the people who usually came into *her* shop were busy buying dog biscuits from Sly Dog and giving him the money for them.

Sly Dog's cap lying on the pavement was full of money — the money that Bossy should have had the fun of counting — but now she wouldn't.

"Sly dog, you *sly dog*!" gasped Bossy. "How dare you say that my daddy's shop is shut, when it isn't?"

Sly Dog looked at her coldly.

"I haven't said that your daddy's shop is shut," he said, and went on selling biscuits.

"But you *have*!" shouted Bossy banging her little paw on Sly Dog's sign. "It says here: The Dog Biscuit Shop is shut."

"Oh yes!" sneered Sly Dog, "but it doesn't say *which* Dog Biscuit Shop. Now if you look at the back of my sign, you will see something else written."

Bossy walked round and looked at the back of the sign — and there — in such tiny writing that it could hardly be seen — let alone read — it said: "I mean the Dog Biscuit shop in the next town, of course."

Sly Dog sneered.

"It's not my fault if people don't bother to read the back of the sign as well as the front is it?" he laughed, "And if people would rather buy my dog biscuits than bother to go and see if your shop is really open or not — then that is just your hard luck, isn't it, Bossy-boots Bossy — so there."

And Sly Dog went on selling biscuits like hot cakes.

Well, of course the next thing Bossy did was to rush to tell her chum Police Dog Dependable what was happening.

But Police Dog said that Sly Dog wasn't doing anything actually against the law and that there was nothing the police could do.

"I will come down and frown at him and take out my notebook and pencil and look as if I might take down his name and address, if you like," said Police Dog Dependable, trying to be helpful.

"That's no use! But thanks all the same!" snapped Bossy, stamping off.

But as Bossy walked back towards the shop, she had an idea.

"Two can play at Sly Dog's game," she grinned to herself.

And a little while later, Sly Dog suddenly noticed that no one was buying his biscuits any more — they were going past him and buying their biscuits in the Dog Biscuit Shop.

At first he couldn't understand what was wrong — then he peeped round the corner and saw Bossy walking up and down carrying a sign.

And on the sign was written in big letters:

"Sly Dog's Biscuits taste NASTY."

Sly Dog was furious.

"My biscuits don't taste nasty at all," he said.

"You haven't read the rest of my sign," smiled Bossy.

And then in tiny writing on the other side of Bossy's sign, Sly Dog read:

"If you put too much pepper on them."

"It's not my fault if people don't read both sides of my sign," grinned Bossy cheekily.

And as Police Dog Dependable came strolling down the road at that moment, Sly Dog decided he had had enough and took his biscuits and went off.

So the rest of the day went well and Bossy had lots of money to count at the end of the day.

"That Sly Dog may be sly," grinned Bossy, "but he isn't sly enough to get the better of me."

Hero to the rescue

One fine sunny day, Gay Dog had been out for a sail in his boat and on his way back had almost reached the shore, when the wind dropped.

Instead of sailing in quickly, Gay Dog's boat lay there rocking gently on the sea and just coming in very slowly on the tide.

Well, Gay Dog wasn't really bothered, because he knew the tide would drift him home in the end, so he settled down to enjoy the sunshine.

But then Gay Dog's brother Hero and his little sister came running down to the beach and shouted to him across the water.

"Dinner will be ready in ten minutes," shouted Hero, "and it is your favourite dinner – shepherd's pie and carrots followed by raspberries and cream."

Gay Dog pricked his ears up at that. He loved shepherd's pie followed by raspberries and cream.

"Yippee!" he shouted. "But tell Mum I won't be home in ten minutes. The wind has dropped – I may not be home for a couple of hours. Ask her to save my share for me."

Bossy laughed. "What a hope!" she shouted. "Shepherd's pie and carrots and raspberries and cream are my favourites, too. If you're not home in time, I will eat my share and yours as well – and serve you right for being late."

Gay Dog was quite annoyed. He didn't really think his mother would let Bossy eat his dinner – but then, who knew what Bossy **might** do when Mummy wasn't looking?

Gay Dog looked round but there was no sign of wind. The sea was as flat as a pancake.

Then Gay Dog **did** see something.

He saw the Merry Mermaid.

The Merry Mermaid was the ship belonging to Sea Dog and it was coming into harbour with its little engine running.

You see, the Merry Mermaid was a sailing ship – like Gay Dog's, but it had an engine as well, for when there was no wind.

"Oh good," thought Gay Dog. "I will

get Sea Dog to give me a pull into harbour." And Gay Dog shouted to Sea Dog: "Ahoy, there, Skipper. Will you tow me into harbour, please?"

Sea Dog chuckled and grinned craftily. "Of course I will. You jump aboard the Merry Mermaid, messmate, and I'll take your dinky little sailing boat in tow."

Gay Dog **was** pleased. He called across the water and told Bossy and Hero what was happening. "And tell Mum I'll be home in time for dinner — and don't you dare touch my share, Bossy, you naughty girl."

Bossy laughed. "We'll see," she grinned and she and Hero turned to go home.

They walked up the hill away from the seashore and were just trotting down the other side towards their home, when they met Police Dog Dependable walking along and pushing his bicycle. "Hallo there," he smiled. "Been sailing with Gay Dog, have you?" "No," smiled Hero in reply, "but we have been talking to him. He is stuck a little way out at sea because there is no wind to blow him into harbour. Sea Dog is towing him in."

"What?" Police Dog Dependable shouted so loudly, that Hero and Bossy almost jumped out of their skins.

"WHAT is Sea Dog going to do?" yelled Police Dog.

"He's taking Gay Dog aboard the Merry Mermaid and towing Gay Dog's boat into harbour!" said Hero.

Police Dog Dependable looked terribly worried. "You know what that means, don't you?" he shouted.

"Yes, I know," said Bossy rubbing her ears, "and there's no need to shout. It means that Gay Dog will be home in time for dinner and I won't be able to eat his shepherd's pie and carrots and raspberries and cream. That's what it means."

"No, it doesn't!" shrieked Police Dog almost dancing on the spot with excitement. "It means that by the time they get into harbour Gay Dog's boat will belong to Sea Dog!"

Bossy and Hero stared at Police Dog Dependable in amazement.

"Look! I think you've been overdoing it," said Bossy kindly. "Why don't you go home and ask Mrs. Police Dog to make you a nice cup of tea with plenty of sugar in it?"

"Oh, don't you understand?" gasped Police Dog. "It is the rule of the sea. If you come across a boat drifting with nobody aboard and bring it into harbour, then it is called 'salvage' and the boat belongs to you. If you don't know that, you can take my word that Sea Dog does."

Bossy looked worried.

"You mean — " she began. Police Dog Dependable nodded.

"Sea Dog has tricked your brother," he said.

Now Hero hadn't been saying much all this time but he had been thinking.

"Someone must get back and warn Gay

Dog not to go aboard the Merry Mermaid," he thought. "Naughty old Sea Dog mustn't get away with his wicked plan."

He looked at Police Dog. "Could I borrow your bicycle and race to warn Gay Dog?" he asked.

"I think you will have to," said Police Dog. "I would go myself but you are younger than I and your nippy little legs will pedal the bicycle along much faster than mine could. But be very careful going down the side of the hill towards the sea. The hill is steep and if you go too fast, you will go straight ahead on to the beach and into the sea."

In a moment Hero had taken the bicycle and raced to the top of the hill.

He looked down — and then — **horrors** — he saw the Merry Mermaid moving close to Gay Dog's boat and Sea Dog was shouting across to Gay Dog.

"I must get there before Gay Dog climbs aboard the Merry Mermaid," thought Hero. "Now is the time for me to live up to my name and be a real hero."

Climbing on to the bicycle, Hero pointed it down the straight road to the beach.

He didn't put the brakes on once and he pedalled as fast as he could go. Like the wind he whizzed along.

Soon he was going so fast he shut his eyes. Then suddenly, the bicycle ploughed into the soft sand of the beach and stopped. Hero was thrown forward and landed — **SPLASH** — in the sea.

He struggled up to the surface and was just in time to call to Gay Dog and stop him from climbing aboard the Merry Mermaid. A few minutes later the wind started to blow again and Gay Dog's boat started to move towards the harbour.

"Hooray!" spluttered Hero. "Gay Dog's boat is saved."

He grinned as he saw Sea Dog fairly dancing with rage because his cunning plan had come to nothing.

Hero struggled out of the sea — and in the end he and Bossy and Gay Dog arrived home for dinner safe and sound.

And guess what?

Mummy had made enough shepherd's pie and carrots and bought enough raspberries and cream for everyone to have second helpings. What a wonderful feast it was!

Mother's Day

It was early one Sunday morning in the home of Mr. and Mrs. Dog Biscuit.

Bossy, the little girl dog, grunted and turned over in bed. She knew it was far too early to get up—and yet—and yet—something was bothering her.

Bossy could hear funny noises coming from downstairs. She sat up in bed and cocked up her ears.

The noises came again.

Squelchity! Squelch!

Bonk! Bonk!

"Gosh!" gasped Bossy. "What a strange noise!"

Bossy's little heart thumped. She slipped out of bed, dragged on her woolly cardigan, and crept on to the landing.

"I'd better wake up Dad" thought Bossy.

And Bossy was just going to creep into her Mummy's and Daddy's room, when another sound came drifting up the stairs.

"Tra-la-la! Hum-tiddle-te-tum!" came the sound. It was the sound of somebody singing. And Bossy knew who that somebody was.

It was her youngest brother Little Diddums.

Down the stairs stomped Bossy and across to the kitchen doorway. And there to her amazement, she saw Little Diddums

He had just finished sweeping and washing the kitchen floor. And now he was laying a tray with the early morning tea and biscuit things. And while he was doing it he was humming.

Bossy gaped at Diddums "Have you gone silly?" she gasped. "What are you doing up so early in the morning? And why have you cleaned the kitchen floor? That's Mum's job!"

Diddums looked round and gave his sister his sweet smile. "Don't you remember what day it is?" he asked.

Bossy looked blank.

"It's Mother's Day," went on Diddums. "I hadn't got any money to buy Mum a present, so I thought I would get up and do some work for her instead."

Bossy still looked surprised.

"Well, I know we are supposed to do things to help on Mother's Day," she said. "But surely we don't have to come down and scrub floors—why, that's hard work."

But Diddums just went on working. "That's the whole idea!" he said. "Just for one day a year—on Mother's Day—we are supposed to do the hard work, so Mum can have an easy time."

Bossy was feeling rather upset because she had forgotten to buy anything or do anything for her mother.

"I don't know why you're laying that tea tray." she said to Diddums. "You can't make any tea to go on it. You know you're not allowed to touch boiling kettles."

Bossy was really sneering—but Diddums didn't mind.

"Oh no—it's all worked out," he said. "When everything is ready and the kettle is boiling, I am going to wake up Hero. He is old enough to touch hot kettles and he can make the tea and we can take it up to Mum together."

Then Little Diddums pointed to an empty vase on the tea tray.

"I haven't forgotten you," he said. "I thought you would like to pick some flowers to go into that vase. Then we three, Hero, you and I can all take the tray up to Mum and wish her happy Mother's Day."

Well, Bossy was really very pleased that she was able to join in being nice to Mum. And she was pleased with Diddums for letting her join in, though she wouldn't admit it.

She pulled on her wellingtons and a raincoat over her cardigan and nightdress and went to pick some wild flowers from the meadow at the bottom of the garden.

So, just as Mummy Dog woke up, into her room trooped Diddums and Bossy and Hero, with a lovely tray of tea and biscuits and a vase of pretty wild flowers.

Mummy **was** pleased! Especially when Diddums said he had cleaned the kitchen floor.

And then Daddy gave Mummy some new gloves and Gay Dog gave his mother a box of chocolates.

And everyone was very happy.

A visit to the warship

"I say! Do you know what I've seen?" shouted Little Diddums, the baby of the Dog family, as he ran indoors, just as everyone was sitting down to lunch.

All the rest of the family — Mummy, Daddy, Gay Dog the eldest brother, Hero the middle brother and Bossy their little sister — looked at Diddums.

"Of course, we don't know," snapped Bossy. "We haven't been with you, so how could we know — you **do** ask stupid questions."

But even a grumpy answer from Bossy couldn't take the shining look out of Diddums' eyes.

"Well," he gasped, "I was riding along in Daddy's Biscuit Shop van, with old Mutt, the driver. We were running along the coast road, and I looked out to sea and I saw a WARSHIP!"

"A WARSHIP!" gasped the rest of the family.

They were really very interested.

"Yes," smiled Diddums. "Old Mutt said it is what is called a destroyer and it had great big guns and it was anchored about a mile out to sea. Old Mutt said he had heard that the ship had stopped to take on food from our harbour and that it would be there **all day**."

Of course everyone was thrilled at the exciting news, but then Gay Dog said he had got to get back to work at the Car Salesrooms, where his job was and Daddy said he had to get back to his dog biscuit shop and Mummy said she had to do the washing up and then the ironing — you know the dull things grown-ups always find for themselves to do.

So that just left the children Hero, Bossy and Diddums.

As soon as lunch was over, they raced down to the harbour.

And when they stood on the harbour wall and looked out to sea — there, about a mile away, they could see a real warship.

How magnificent it was!

Scurrying about on deck were the tiny figures of the sailors in their blue uniforms.

"I wish I could get a close look at it," sighed Hero.

"So do I," sighed Bossy.

"Me, too," sighed Diddums.

But then suddenly, who should come striding down to the harbour, but Sea Dog.

Now Sea Dog had heard about the warship being anchored out at sea and it had given him an idea to make money.

He set up a board at the side of his ship, the Merry Mermaid and he painted on the board in big black letters:

"Trips to see the warship — 10p."

The children's eyes nearly popped out of their heads.

"Would you really take us out to see the warship?" they asked Sea Dog.

"Of course," he smiled, "so long as you have ten pence each — and I want to see your money before we go."

Bossy gave a big grin.

"Oh, don't worry about the money," she said, fetching out her purse and showing Sea Dog that she had **sixty** pence in it. "I've been saving up my pocket money to buy some doll's clothes, but now I would rather spend ten pence of it on going to see the warship and I will pay for my brothers to go, too, and they can pay me back when they get their pocket money."

Bossy was always rather bossy when she talked, but really she was a good sort and she didn't want her brothers to miss the chance of a trip round the warship.

So Bossy gave Sea Dog thirty pence — that was ten pence each — and they scrambled into the Merry Mermaid and set sail.

Little Diddums did mutter something about, "Don't you think we should ask Mummy first?"

But Bossy pushed him quickly into the boat.

"By the time we have gone home and asked Mummy and then got back here, the warship might have gone," she said. "Don't be a scaredy boots. Anyway, what can be wrong? We have known Sea Dog for years, haven't we? And he may be naughty and up to all sorts of crafty tricks now and then,

but he would never allow us to come to any harm."

So out they sailed to the warship.

It was wonderful seeing it close to, with its big guns and its radio masts and the sailors working aboard.

The sailors even waved to the children and called out and asked them their names.

It **was** thrilling.

But then at last, it got to be near teatime and Bossy said,

"Well, that was lovely, thanks, Sea Dog, but I think it is time to go back now."

Sea Dog sat comfortably on a seat at the stern of his boat.

"Oh, you want me to take you **back** do you?" he said, with a sly look on his face. "In that case that will be another ten pence each, please, Miss Bossy."

The children stared at him.

"But we have already paid ten pence each for our trip," said Hero.

"Oh, you've paid ten pence each to see the warship," sneered Sea Dog, "but my notice didn't say anything about taking you back again. If you want me to take you **back** again, that will be another ten pence each, **please**."

Bossy was furious.

"I won't pay you, you cheat!" she snapped.

Sea Dog just sat back more comfortably on his seat.

"Please yourself, Miss Bossy," he said. "If you don't want me to take you back, just nip over the side and swim and you had better start straight away if you want to be home in time for tea."

Bossy wriggled with rage, but she looked at the cold sea and she knew that she would

have to pay the money.

"You've tricked us, you horrid thing!" she said, as she handed her last thirty pence over to Sea Dog.

"Yes, I have, haven't I?" laughed Sea Dog, feeling very pleased with himself. "That will teach you to flash your money about and let people see how much you have in your purse."

So back they sailed to the harbour with the three children feeling very glum.

It was lucky for them that Police Dog Dependable happened to be at the harbour when they got back.

Bossy told him at once what had happened. Police Dog Dependable frowned.

But Sea Dog wasn't bothered.

"My sign says '**Trips to see the warship — 10p**' he yawned. "It doesn't say anything about being brought back afterwards."

And really he was right.

Police Dog thought for a moment.

Then he said, "Ah, Sea Dog, but have you a **licence** for taking people on trips?"

Sea Dog blinked and scratched his head.

"You see, going out sailing in your own ship is one thing," explained Police Dog, "but if you make people pay to go for a sail, then you have to have a licence."

Sea Dog started to look worried.

"Well, what do I do now?"

Police Dog smiled.

"You tried to cheat Miss Bossy out of thirty pence," he said. "Give it back to her and I won't report you. But you must buy a licence tomorrow."

Sea Dog muttered and grumbled but he handed back the thirty pence to Bossy who couldn't stop chuckling.

Then Sea Dog stamped away angrily.

"Thank you, Police Dog Dependable" said Bossy and Hero and Diddums. Isn't Police Dog Dependable a splendid chap?

Bossy and the Cherry Tree

Now at the bottom of the dog family's garden was a cherry tree.

One year there were lots of cherries on the tree.

Bossy, the little girl dog, who loved eating cherries, was longing for the day when the cherries would be ripe and she could eat them.

Every day she used to go down to look at the cherry tree.

"When will the cherries be ripe, Daddy?" she would ask.

"In a few days, in a few days," Daddy would reply.

But then Bossy noticed that the garden birds seemed to be taking a great interest in the cherry tree, too.

Every time Bossy went down to look at the cherries to see if they were ripe, the birds were looking at them as well.

Bossy grew suspicious.

"Daddy," she said, "do birds by any chance like eating cherries?"

Daddy laughed.

"Do birds like eating cherries?" he chuckled. "I should **say they** do. They just **love** them."

Well, at last the day arrived, when Daddy Dog said, "Bossy! The cherries will be ready to eat tomorrow morning."

"Lovely," said Bossy.

"And now," she went on, "I will go out and **tell** those birds that they mustn't eat the cherries, because they are for us, our family and especially me."

Daddy sighed.

"You can **tell** the birds," he said, "but I don't suppose they will take any notice of you."

Bossy looked quite cross.

"Do you mean to say that they will eat **the cherries** after I have told them they belong to us," she said, in surprise.

Daddy Dog nodded.

"The birds think they can eat just anything they see," he said.

"Oh, well then," said Bossy, "I will go down straight after breakfast tomorrow and tell them to keep away."

Daddy sighed again.

"I'm afraid after breakfast will be too late," he said. "Birds always get up at dawn. They will be eating the cherries long before you are even awake. That is why year after year we never get many cherries. Those birds eat them before we are up in the morning."

Bossy was upset.

"How rotten!" she said.

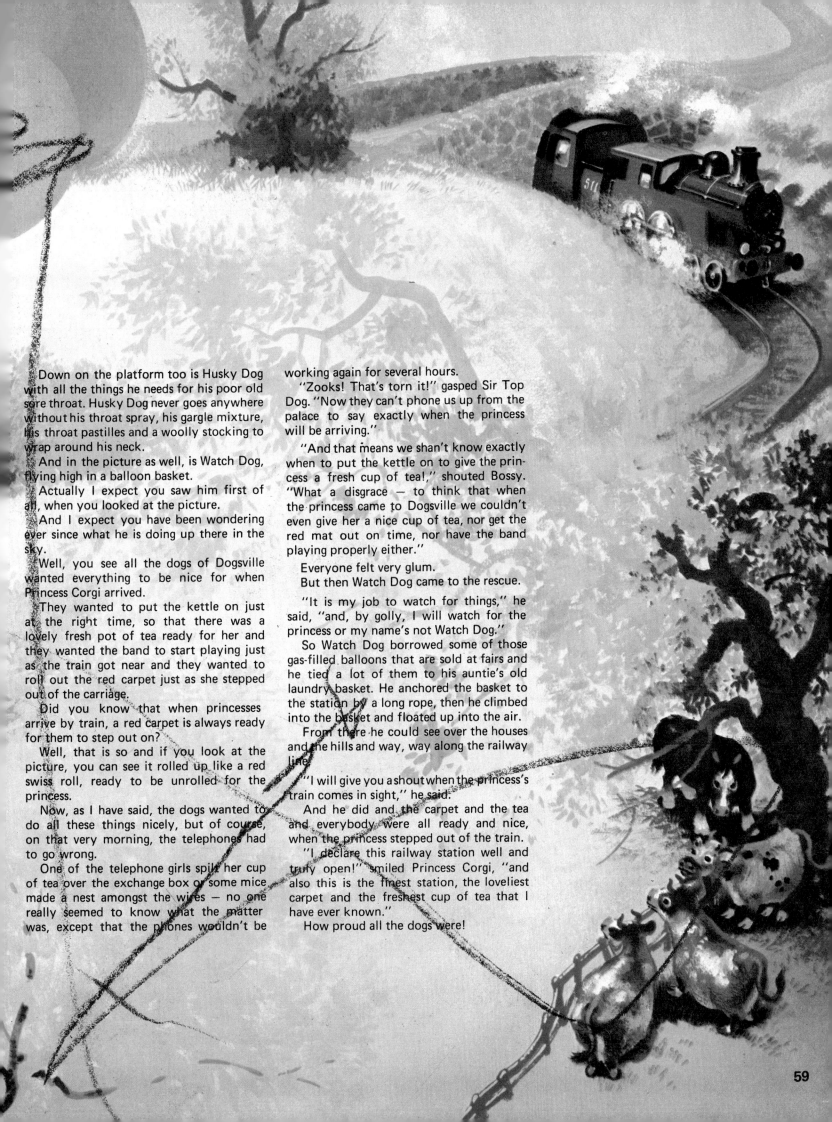

Down on the platform too is Husky Dog with all the things he needs for his poor old sore throat. Husky Dog never goes anywhere without his throat spray, his gargle mixture, his throat pastilles and a woolly stocking to wrap around his neck.

And in the picture as well, is Watch Dog, flying high in a balloon basket.

Actually I expect you saw him first of all, when you looked at the picture.

And I expect you have been wondering ever since what he is doing up there in the sky.

Well, you see all the dogs of Dogsville wanted everything to be nice for when Princess Corgi arrived.

They wanted to put the kettle on just at the right time, so that there was a lovely fresh pot of tea ready for her and they wanted the band to start playing just as the train got near and they wanted to roll out the red carpet just as she stepped out of the carriage.

Did you know that when princesses arrive by train, a red carpet is always ready for them to step out on?

Well, that is so and if you look at the picture, you can see it rolled up like a red swiss roll, ready to be unrolled for the princess.

Now, as I have said, the dogs wanted to do all these things nicely, but of course, on that very morning, the telephones had to go wrong.

One of the telephone girls spilt her cup of tea over the exchange box or some mice made a nest amongst the wires — no one really seemed to know what the matter was, except that the phones wouldn't be working again for several hours.

"Zooks! That's torn it!" gasped Sir Top Dog. "Now they can't phone us up from the palace to say exactly when the princess will be arriving."

"And that means we shan't know exactly when to put the kettle on to give the princess a fresh cup of tea!," shouted Bossy. "What a disgrace — to think that when the princess came to Dogsville we couldn't even give her a nice cup of tea, nor get the red mat out on time, nor have the band playing properly either."

Everyone felt very glum.

But then Watch Dog came to the rescue.

"It is my job to watch for things," he said, "and, by golly, I will watch for the princess or my name's not Watch Dog."

So Watch Dog borrowed some of those gas-filled balloons that are sold at fairs and he tied a lot of them to his auntie's old laundry basket. He anchored the basket to the station by a long rope, then he climbed into the basket and floated up into the air.

From there he could see over the houses and the hills and way, way along the railway line.

"I will give you a shout when the princess's train comes in sight," he said.

And he did and the carpet and the tea and everybody were all ready and nice, when the princess stepped out of the train.

"I declare this railway station well and truly open!" smiled Princess Corgi, "and also this is the finest station, the loveliest carpet and the freshest cup of tea that I have ever known."

How proud all the dogs were!

At the end of the rainbow

It was one of those showery sunny days, when, if you were lucky, you could see a lovely rainbow in the sky.

Well, Little Diddums, was lucky. He looked across from the back garden of his home and saw a beautiful rainbow stretching over the river and down into the meadows.

"How pretty!" he gasped.

Then he called to his sister, Bossy: "Come and look at this, Bossy!"

Bossy came dashing out.

"What stupid thing are you bothering me about now..... Oh golly! How lovely!"

The rainbow was so beautiful, that for a moment, even Bossy stopped talking.

She looked at the end of the rainbow going down into the meadows.

"I say," she murmured, "it isn't often that you see the end of a rainbow like that."

Diddums looked at the end of the rainbow, too.

"In those fairy stories that Mummy reads to us at bedtime," he said, "it says that there is a pot of gold at the end of the rainbow."

"Hmmm! Surely you don't believe in that rubbish!" sniffed Bossy. "Pot of gold my foot. All you are likely to find if you go down into the meadows is a bootful of mud!"

Diddums sighed.

"I suppose you're right," he said, "but you never know. Sometimes fairy stories do come true."

Diddums looked at the beautiful rainbow again.

"Well, I don't care whether you say it is rubbish or not," he said. "I'm going down to the end of the rainbow just to check up on whether there **is** anything there."

He pulled on his wellingtons and told Mummy where he was going and set off.

The children were allowed to go to the meadows on their own, as they were in sight of the house.

Bossy watched Diddums go.

"Silly little mutt!" she muttered.

But then she thought — "Just suppose — just suppose he **does** find some gold at the end of the rainbow! I shall feel an awful fool if Diddums comes back rich and I'm still here with nothing but twenty pence in my money box."

Suddenly she dragged on her wellingtons, called through the kitchen door: "Just going to the meadows with Diddums, Mum" and she was off down the lane after Diddums.

Brother and sister plodded along down to the meadows, and although Diddums guessed that Bossy was coming, because

she **did** really half believe in the gold, he was too kind to say so.

Now all this time, back in the house, Mummy Dog had been in the kitchen making sausage rolls and cakes for tea.

She had heard Diddums and Bossy talking about the gold at the end of the rainbow and as she watched their two little figures plodding down to the meadows, she did feel sorry for them.

"They will go all the way down there — get muddy boots, search around — find nothing and then come back so disappointed," she thought. "I wish I could do something about it — I hate to see them upset."

Then Mummy had an idea.

She remembered some gold wrapping paper she had saved from Christmas.

"I will make two pots of gold for them to find at the end of the rainbow," she smiled.

And Mummy took two little pudding basins, put some hot sausage-rolls and hot cakes in each of them and then wrapped them up in the pretty gold paper.

Then she called her eldest son, Gay Dog.

"Here, Gay Dog" said Mummy, "do me a big favour. Please drive down to the meadows and take these two gold parcels. Run into the meadows and put the the parcels as near as you can to the end

of the rainbow. Then slip back home as fast as you can."

Bossy and Diddums noticed Gay Dog zipping past and then coming back again, but they didn't think much about it. Gay Dog was always zipping somewhere.

Gay Dog was always dashing about leading his gay life.

So it happened that when the two little dogs squelched their way across the meadows, what should they see plop in the middle of the field, but two pots of gold.

"Look!" gasped Diddums. "What did I tell you?"

Bossy was so amazed she could not speak at all.

They snatched up a pot of gold each and tore off the paper.

Well, of course, it was just a little disappointing that there was no gold inside, but the lovely hot sausage-rolls and cakes looked really yummy.

Bossy and Diddums ran all the way home full of excitement at their find.

And when Mummy said it was all right to eat the rolls and cakes, they had a lovely tuck-in.

For days they kept talking about what they had found at the end of the rainbow — they were so happy.

And every time they talked about the pots of gold, Mummy and Gay Dog just smiled and said nothing.

Have you ever seen a rainbow — or the end of a rainbow — or even a pot of gold?

Perhaps you will one day.

ISBN 0 85988 003 6

GAY DOG

HERO

WATCH DOG

HUSKY DOG

SEA DOG